Stranded

SUNRISE ISLAND BROTHERS 2

E. DAVIES

Publisher's Note: This is a work of fiction. Names, characters, places, and incidents are a product of the author's imagination. Locales and public names are sometimes used for atmospheric purposes. Any resemblance to actual people, living or dead, or to businesses, companies, events, institutions, or locales is completely coincidental.

Stranded / E. Davies. – 1st ed.
978-1-912245-25-3

Stranded

Prologue

RONAN

"THIS IS THE LAST TRIP OF THE NIGHT," THE SKIPPER'S VOICE crackles over the tinny intercom. His eyes land on me as he pointedly adds, "I hope nobody's here by accident."

The passengers around us chuckle, and my cheeks burn with defiance. I fold my arms and stare right back at him.

They're not wrong. I couldn't stand out more if I tried.

Everyone else is dressed like they're hoping to escape the day-to-day and discover their soul's purpose on Maple Island. They're heading to the campground carrying tents, picnic coolers, camping chairs, hiking boots—you name it, they've got it.

And then there's me.

I'm wearing black, faux leather short-shorts, a sheer, glittery gold top, and black sneakers. At the last moment, I threw on a hoodie—black, hand-detailed in a pattern of gold fans and dots.

Where I'm going, I won't need more than that.

Ooh, that's cold!

I shiver as a breeze blows in from the harbour, right across the back of my neck. It might still be summer, but the sun is setting earlier and earlier as August draws to a close. There's a nip in the air.

The skipper's brows creep toward his hairline, and I blush as I zip up my hoodie, then tuck my hands back into the sleeves.

After a long pause, the skipper shrugs and turns away. "Keep everything safe and secure, please, folks," he shouts over the engine as he works on the ferry ropes. "Especially tents and stealthy brown-bagged bottles."

A sigh of relief rushes from my lungs as I tune him out and stare across the water.

It's not like I'm ashamed.

Grindr is a perfectly natural part of human existence. Humans wouldn't have evolved thumbs if they didn't want horny, dumb young guys to use them to do crazy things.

Like saying *yes* when a guy I've been texting for a day invites me to join him for a hot night under the stars.

After the last couple of days, there's nothing I need more than a night of mindless fun. Otherwise, I'll just keep replaying it in my mind every time I try to close my eyes.

Family dinner, the forced conversation, the careful pause, and finally... the ultimatum.

Improve my grades by the end of the semester, or else they won't pay for the January semester.

Without it, I can't get my BA in Fashion Design. I'll probably have to follow in my brothers' dress shoe-shaped footprints... all the way to the family accounting firm.

They told me there's a job waiting for me, but I already know it'll be something that sucks the creative life force right out of me. I'll have to put on a badly-fitted suit for a job

I haven't earned, pushing papers I don't understand… and it gets worse.

I'll be cursed with enough knowledge to understand why the suits fit so badly.

Okay, fine… I could quietly tailor them myself. The point is, the whole premise flies in the face of everything I've ever designed for—or fought for, or *lived* for.

I've been styling outfits from the day I could walk in my mom's high heels. I altered everything in sight until my family started hiding their clothes and taking me to Value Village for sacrificial clothing.

Everyone knows this is what I was born to do; they just don't believe I'm good enough.

But I know better.

I can do anything I want—and I'm starting with this nameless guy. I'm gonna do him all damn night, thank you very much.

Then I'll figure out how to put together my first mini-collection, earn my way back into the good graces of the infamous Professor Meyer, and get the best work experience placement of all.

XX Gracieux.

It's a new brand, but they've poached some serious talent from household names. They're edgy, modern, eye-catching—like punk meets runway, but dripping with sex appeal.

I'd kill to get a placement there… and so would my whole class.

Only one of us will get that offer. Some of us will get decent placements… but for those of us at the bottom of the class, it'll be a few long months of sweeping floors. Wherever Professor Meyer thinks we'll fit in best.

Based on my grades right now, I might as well start warming up my sweeping muscles.

The mainland slowly shrinks behind us, until we're passing Sunrise Island. Some of the island's residents wave to us from their back porches or the beach, and I can't help a smile as I join the other passengers and wave back.

But my gaze is fixed on the other island of the pair—Maple. The whole island is a park, so apart from the visitor centre, museum building, cafe, and campground, there's just forests and beaches.

I can smell barbecues, though I can't tell if it's coming from Sunrise or Maple. Is one of those scents my dinner tonight?

My stomach grumbles, and I bite back a grin as I turn my face into the breeze, shrugging off the cold as anticipation builds in my chest.

I pull out my phone again to reread my favourite part of the conversation with my date—a profile named *IslandHeat*.

Wow. Not a lot of guys in your industry are this smart, hot, and single.

I don't want to wait to meet you.

Can I treat you to dinner tonight? Please?

Wow okay thanks um

Haha assuming you aren't being sarcastic

But you said you're camping??

Will you come join me? Campfire dinner, wine on the beach, and stargazing while you tell me all about the artistic dreams you want to make come true.

And then we can fuck all night.

(But quietly. Respecting my camping
neighbours.)

(Okay, respect is optional and may be
thrown out the window)

Are you there?

> Are you serious?? I don't even know you.

Phew. But you'll only get to know me by
saying yes.

Please?

> OK. I'll come.

OMG I can't believe you said yes! Are you
really coming?

> Really really. Maybe our dreams can come
> true...

Mine already have.

As the ferry bumps the dock, I quickly scroll down to the bottom. No new messages, so I thumb-peck one of my own.

> I'm here. Where are you?

Then I pocket my phone, my nostrils full of the smell of seaweed and diesel and trees.

We get off the ferry, and it really starts to sink in when I reach the end of the wharf. I wait for my turn to climb the steep ramp as we all file past the lineup of people waiting to board.

This is really the last sailing. It's not too late—I could still change my mind.

But then I'd miss my chance to get laid. No way. I need this.

My heart is pounding and my mouth is dry, and I want to tell myself it's all horniness, but it's not. I'm nervous as hell for what sounds like not just a hookup but… a date.

What better to break through a creative drought?

Uninspired, my professors called my work. *Derivative. D-worthy.*

Kind of like my Grindr hookups over the last few years. But this one sounds different.

"Gonna camp right here?" someone behind me asks.

"Oh. Shit, sorry." It's my turn, so I clutch the handrail and climb—up, up, and a little more up.

I'm winded by the time I step through the gate and onto the hillside. There's a map of the island ahead, decorated with little trails snaking off in different directions.

Until my mysterious date responds, I don't know where to go.

The ferry blows its whistle as I tap out another message.

> Are you coming to meet me or…?

The other campers head off toward the campground in little groups, while I stay, fighting the urge to glance back at the ferry and run for it.

Everything is going to be fine, right?

Unless *this* is the time my Grindr hookup ghosts me. Or catfishes me. Or turns out to be a mountain man-turned-serial killer… I listen to podcasts. I know what's up.

Or he's perfectly normal.

Or… this is a real possibility… *he's* perfectly normal, but neither of us know about the real serial killer hiding in the woods.

I almost jump out of my skin when something moves on my screen.

...

Three dots. That means he's typing.

"Thank God," I breathe out, smoothing a hand down my front as I turn on the spot to look for him.

I'm half-expecting a message being like, *Are you the guy in wildly impractical clothing standing by the dock?*

He stops and starts typing a few times, and I click my tongue with impatience.

Maybe he can't come meet me. Like… he's grilling food for me ahead of my arrival. Now, *that* would be romantic.

A boy can dream, right?

Share your location?

He shares the map right away, and I tap it to open it full-screen.

But it's not working right. It's showing me where I was when I first messaged him—the pin is on my street, and directly on my house.

I shake my phone with frustration, barely resisting the urge to throw the damn thing in the harbour. "Fuck this app and fuck its glitches," I groan.

Then I take a deep breath and calm down enough to open up the conversation again.

Get it yet?

> Yeah but it's showing the wrong place for some reason .

> Hahahahahahahahahaha

I freeze, my lips slowly parting as I stare at his laughter. Fear trails down my spine like a fingertip, slow and icy cold.

This *is* some freaky serial killer shit. Is he doing this to freak me out? What if he's really at my house?

But... he shouldn't know where I live.

Wait a minute. I can look at the grid of nearby users. Unless there's a Maple Island Pride festival I don't know about, I should see anyone on these islands within the first screen or two of little square profile pictures.

I fumble and tap out of the conversation, swiping away the notification about some other profile hitting on me.

"Sorry, SuckMeXXL. Not a good moment."

I skim the first few dozen profiles, but my date isn't there. "*Shiiiiiiit.*"

There's no sign of anyone between me and the campground.

The ferry is well and truly gone.

And there's a new photo from IslandHeat. I hold my breath as I tap to open it.

Oh, fuck.

I close my eyes slowly, my cheeks burning as the ground threatens to swallow me whole.

Why didn't I see this coming?

Because it's the kind of thing only a real, *real* asshole would do. Or a whole group of them—like my roommates.

Derek, Shane, and Breanna are huddled together on the couch. Derek is holding the phone, but he's laughing his ass off so much that he can't even hold it steady for the photo.

This was all a prank. The worst prank in the world.

"Holy *fuck*," I whisper, fury rising in my chest. "What the hell?"

My classmates are spoiled brats who enjoy rubbing their straight As in my face, and making me the butt of all their jokes. They pretend I'm not in the room when they talk about the clothing line they're planning to launch together. Hell, they've rented a studio together for the business, and they've never even offered to show me around.

I've sucked it up until now because I have a huge room and the rent is cheap, but... they've never gone this far before.

> I can't believe you bought all that artistic
> dream crap
>
> What's the matter
>
> Is it your grades??
>
> hahahaha
>
> I'd offer to call the coast guard
>
> but idk man, you might be a bad-luck charm
> and sink them too
>
> like your career

"As if," I snort, my cheeks flushed with fury. I'd rather get eaten by bears than beg for their help.

I block the profile, close the app, and stare down the challenge on my screen.

Delete this app and all its data?

"Fuck, yes." I tap my screen to do it. Then, I shove my phone in my pocket as I walk down to the beach to look around for anyone I could call for help.

Whatever lies ahead, I'll find a way through—all by myself.

I've never been so scared. But there's something fresh and clear about the anger simmering in my veins. I haven't felt this way since the family dinner. Hell, since the end of the last semester.

I feel... hopeful.

CHAPTER

One

ALPH

I've always had a pretty solid gut instinct, but it's usually busy sending me weirdly specific warnings.

Hey, dumbass, are you actually going to move to Alberta because you're trying to convince yourself that you're in love? How's that gonna work out for you?

Making good life decisions has been a nice change, and it all started when I moved back to Sunrise Island two months ago.

Now my instinct gets to tell me *good* stuff sometimes. Right now, I have the feeling that a walk home along the beach is exactly what I need.

I'm one of the skippers of the public ferry. It's the end of my shift, and the sun is already setting. If I hurry, I'll get the best view ever—the perfect end to the perfect day.

There's only one factor I can't control: my boss, Berty, and his motor mouth.

As I step into the island's only restaurant, the bartender flutters his fingers in a greeting wave. "Back from your travels?" Kieran grins. "Did they take you anywhere exciting?"

"Sure. Right here to you."

I don't really mind the flirtation; we both know it doesn't mean anything. I'm straight, and he isn't actually interested. But it's nice to end the work day by laughing.

Kieran swoons against the bar top, propping his chin on his hands. "Oh!" he flutters his lashes at me. "Prince Charming has arrived! Are you here to rescue me from a life of cleaning and drudgery?"

I wink at him and slide the boat keys across the counter. "Sorry, man. My heart's already taken—by the sexy little piece of lasagna in my fridge."

Kieran heaves a big sigh and straightens up to put the keys back on the hook. "Damn. Worth a try."

I reach over the bar and clap him on the shoulder. "Don't worry. I'll send any and all poor unsuspecting princes to try on the glass slipper."

Kieran holds up a finger. "Rich unsuspecting princes," he tells me. "And that's not how the story goes. The prince doesn't wear the slipper, I do."

"Don't be so closed-minded. It's a modern world," I tell him, and he sputters at me. "Hey, is Berty around?"

He clicks his tongue and jerks a thumb over his shoulder. "In the kitchen, wise guy. Want me to call him?"

Now, *that's* giving as good as he gets.

"God, no." *Shit. That was a little fast, wasn't it?* "Uh..." I cough sheepishly into my fist. "I mean, nah. That's fine."

Kieran snorts with laughter. He's not from Sunrise Island —his thick Irish accent makes that much obvious—and he's only worked here for a couple weeks.

But that's long enough to learn what everyone knows about our boss. If Berty corners you, the sun will set—and rise again—before you get a word in edgewise.

"Hey, Berty! All done for the night. See you tomorrow," I call out, nodding good night to Kieran on my way out the door.

From here, it's a quick scramble down the path to the shore, and then I stop dead in my tracks.

"Holy shit."

Despite its name, Sunrise Island gets pretty damn good sunsets too.

The sun has dipped below the mountains, sending waves of crimson and gold across the shimmering sky. The neighbouring islands are fading from lively green shapes to black silhouettes smudged against the orange horizon.

It's breathtaking. And only one thing is missing—one thing that would make the moment perfect.

Someone to share it with.

"Not this again," I mumble to myself, running my fingers through my hair. It's too late to shake off the thought—or the bone-deep ache that comes with it.

Loneliness.

"Home," I say out loud to snap myself out of it.

Speaking of snapping, the last thing I need is a twisted ankle in this fading light. With summer drawing to a close, the sunset is earlier every day. There's only just enough light left to safely scramble across the beach.

Keeping my gaze fixed on the stones underfoot, I set off in a steady but careful stride while my thoughts race recklessly ahead.

What would my friends say?

"Stop being such a dumbass," I mumble, rolling my eyes as I picture the exasperated looks on their faces. "If you want to date someone, go on a date."

They'd be right, too. But the thought of swiping right

endlessly until I find a nice woman to go on a perfectly respectable date with...

It doesn't loosen the knot in my chest. If anything, the ache is getting worse.

"Ugh. At least I'll always have lasagna... wait."

Shit.

I trail off and stumble to a halt, squinting through the deepening gloom. I don't even know what I'm looking for, but I've been a big brother my whole life, so I know this feeling.

Someone's in trouble.

There!

I squint across the strait at Maple Island, and I find the reason I stopped. There's a guy walking erratically back and forth along the shoreline.

And, uh... that's a lot of bare skin.

Either he has a weird-ass mosquito kink or he missed the last ferry. My money's on the second one. But whatever the case, the stranger on the other side of the water is stripping naked right here in front of me.

The only thing separating us is a few hundred feet of open water, and the sudden darkness that slipped in while I was distracted—hiding everything but his silhouette.

The really weird part is how I'm reacting to that silhouette. A hot flush rises under my collar, and then it turns into a tingle that sweeps across my skin until all my muscles are tensed up.

And that's not all.

I'm getting hard. *Real* hard. The kind that suddenly I can't stop myself doing something about. If I weren't in public, I guarantee my hand would already be down my pants.

Unfortunately, I am, so my dick is pushing a painful tent against my thick jeans and I can't do anything about it.

"Fuck," I groan, wincing. "What the hell is going on?"

I don't know how to explain the sudden fire in my blood—or the dizzying whirlwind of emotions. I feel excited in a way I haven't for so long, and worried about where the hell this came from, and… well, just plain confused.

In all dates I've been on with women—or even the few attempts at relationships, ending quickly and disastrously—I've never felt *this*. But I've also never tried dating men.

Was *that* the answer all along?

Shit. I should go.

Rush home, jerk off, and forget about this. Not hang out here, staring across the water at this poor stranger like *he's* my lasagna. But I can't tear my gaze away, and I don't even know why.

Adrenaline? Can adrenaline do this?

It's a theory. Worrying about someone in danger, thinking about being lonely, all in the middle of a months-long dry spell… I could almost believe it.

But I can't ignore the throbbing pulse of my downstairs brain. Words *and* coherent thoughts are suddenly hard to come by. And it's only getting harder—in every possible way.

"Oh, *shit*."

Gravel scrapes underfoot as I shift from foot to foot. I'm trying to see better through the gloom.

So I can see more of this naked man who probably doesn't even know I'm watching him.

"Jesus fuck. Alphonso Harris," I breathe out. "Get it together."

I'm not a perv, I swear. However flustered and horny I

am, I can't forget the knot of worry sitting heavily in my belly.

"Aghhhhh—!"

The stranger's cry echoes across the water as he flails around, and I hiss through clenched teeth. He definitely tried to put a toe in the water.

Is he trying to… swim?

He yells again. The sound shatters the night and shakes me to the core. I don't need to hear his actual words in order to know what he's feeling.

Despair.

That's the sound of someone who's in pain—and who feels totally alone.

"Oh, shit," I breathe out, clenching my fist against my chest.

I have to get to him.

It's not even a choice. There's no world in which I could forget about this, and keep walking home to eat lasagna like nothing happened.

I'm sprinting back the way I came, as fast as I possibly can.

There's a lot of unknowns: who this guy is, how he ended up having a breakdown on this beach, or why one look at him made me question everything I've ever assumed about myself.

But I do know two things.

First, he's stranded.

And second, I doubt I can really be his Prince Charming, whatever my body has to say about it… but nothing will stop me from rescuing him.

CHAPTER
Two

RONAN

So far, my experience on Maple Island has only confirmed that I should never apply for Survivor.

I don't know how to build a beach hut, start a fire, or swim more than ten feet without a hot lifeguard's supervision. I could find a stranger in a random tent to ask for help… but that would mean taking the risk of serial killers all over again.

No way am I spending a night sleeping on the beach wearing nothing—or as close as legally possible to it, anyway.

I'm shivering in the cool ocean breeze, so I zip up my hoodie again, folding my arms tightly around my midriff.

"Okay, Ronan. Think," I whisper aloud as I pick my way back up the rocky shore where it's a little warmer. There's always someone nearby—even in those stupid survival shows… "Oh! The ranger station!"

I rush back the way I came, toward the big, bird-poo-covered map at the top of the hill.

The rangers could give me a ride! Or an emergency

blanket and a tent, at least. Even if they're going to laugh at my whole story.

I came here on the last ferry for a hot Grindr date, but someone else turned out to be catfishing me...

My cheeks burn at how stupid it sounds, even in my head. I've gotta make up something better than that.

No fucking way can I tell them the truth.

It's not that I'm ashamed of the hot Grindr date. Only that I was stupid enough to rely on anyone else—especially a stranger—to take care of me.

Well, I've learned that lesson.

I'm looking after myself from now on. And tonight, that means swallowing my pride and asking for help... even if it means making a total ass of myself.

I'll find the ranger station, give them the saddest lost puppy eyes of my life, and then worry about how to kill my roommates—

Wait.

I can't see the water from the hill that leads to the wharf, but I just heard something. My heart leaps damn near out of my throat as I catch my breath and listen.

It's an engine sound. And I swear it's getting louder.

"Holy shit!"

I sprint up the hill, my thighs burning as I curse my allergy to the campus gym.

"Come on," I breathe out when I finally make it to the top of the hill. "Please be my saviour."

I can see movement. A candy-striped pink awning, lit up by the glow of a... headlight? Or whatever the fuck you call the lamp on the bow.

To me, it's a beacon of mercy.

This isn't the boat I took to get here... but it *is* the ferry that goes to Sunrise Island. And at this point, I'd take a stand-up paddle board.

"Here! Come here!" I'm jumping up and down and waving my arms in the dark, yelling to someone who's getting deafened by that old engine.

Real good strategy there. For fuck's sake, Ronan. Just get your ass down to them!

Breathless with excitement—and, to be honest, that stupid hill—I fumble with the heavy iron gate. I wrench it open and trot down the steep ramp to the dock below as the gate bangs closed behind me.

I didn't have to worry about flagging the boat down; regardless of the schedule printed on peeling white paint above the gates, it's clearly heading straight here.

"Oh my god oh my god oh my god," I breathe out.

Silence rings in my ears as the engine suddenly cuts out, while the boat keeps travelling toward the dock with alarming momentum.

"Hey. Back up a little, all right?"

The guy's voice carries a kind of take-charge attitude that makes me shiver right down to the tips of my toes. But that doesn't mean I'm going to listen to him.

I'm teetering on the edge of the dock like an excitable puppy. If I have to plead my case, I will. I'll lie, if that works better. Hell, I'll board the ferry like a freaking pirate—or the slutty Halloween version of a pirate.

"Back?" I echo my possible-rescuer.

He bends to grab something off the floor of the boat as the nose of the ferry touches the wharf. The boat starts to pivot away, and I find myself just talking faster.

"I-I'm sorry. I just want a ride. I'll explain! Please don't leave me stranded—"

"Whoa, whoa," he says. "Easy there. I'm not going to."

There's a real warmth in the voice breaking the darkness. He's not confused or annoyed at me or anything.

Thud.

The skipper just tossed a whole coil of rope my way, but before I can even flinch away, it's already hit its mark. The lasso is snaked perfectly around the cleat just a few feet away from me.

"Oh. Duh." My cheeks are burning as I sheepishly shuffle out of the way—not that it helps now. He just wanted me out of the way for a minute… not forever. "*Back.*"

"Yeah. Lucky for you, I spend a lot of time playing with this rope."

Well, *that's* an opportunity for innuendo if I've ever heard one.

I clamp my mouth shut, trying to keep my giggle inside as the man on the boat hauls on the rope like it weighs nothing, his biceps bulging out of his T-shirt. Then the boat gently bumps the wharf.

I'm finally face-to-face with my rescuer, and… holy shit, he's gorgeous.

The guy's in his mid-twenties, with short brown hair and a jawline that's sharp as hell. I can't tell the colour of his eyes, but they crinkle with a soft amusement that makes me instantly feel better about everything.

In fact, it's his whole energy. I don't think I've seen him before in my life, but I trust him.

I feel… safe.

"You looked lost," the skipper says with a grin, still holding onto the rope. "Need a lift?"

"Oh my god thank you yeah, I—" my stream-ofconsciousness suddenly shuts off as my brain kicks in. He said *looked* lost? "Wait. You saw me on the beach?"

He answers without hesitation. "Yeah."

What the hell did I do down there? I mean… I know exactly what I did. I'm just hoping I did something *else* that warranted rescuing. Maybe he saw me screaming in frustration or pacing back and forth.

Or… maybe he saw me strip naked and test the water.

I duck my head so I can peek up at him through my eyelashes, tugging my hoodie zipper down a little bit. "*All* of me on the beach?"

"Well…" the guy trails off, watching me thoughtfully.

Thoughtful? Not a well-known recipe for Hot Sexy Sailor Time. But at least he isn't making fun of me, so I'm going to choose to cling to hope. Maybe he saw something he liked, and he's here to rescue me *and* my hopes of getting laid.

"Mmhmm?"

The skipper finally clears his throat. "Uh… I don't know how long you were there."

I laugh. He should win an award for the most chivalrous way to say, 'Yes, I definitely saw you stripping naked and running around like you're having a real low point in your life.'

"So…" He's still holding the rope in one strong hand as he offers me the other. "Want a ride?"

"Yes," I breathe out. "Fuck, yes."

Whatever kind of ride I can get.

CHAPTER
Three

ALPH

"HERE. JUST BE CAREFUL—"

Too late.

The overexcitable young man is so eager to get on board that he misses the threshold step completely. I let go of the rope, trying to grab his other arm, but momentum is already winning.

He's about to trip over his own two feet right in front of me... and all I can do is catch him.

"Fuck—!"

The ferry gently sways underneath us as he crashes into me. He's a few inches shorter than me, and built all willowy and slender. For a big, strong guy like me, it's easy to keep him upright.

What I didn't expect was our faces to turn toward each other at the same moment.

His mouth catches the edge of my jaw, then slides up toward the corner of my mouth. I'm rooted to the spot, transfixed by the red-hot sparks dragging along my skin in the wake of his warm, soft lips.

What... the hell... is happening?

My head turns toward his—and I want to tell myself it's out of sheer surprise, but it's not, I know it's *not*—and then our lips meet.

In my experience, kisses—especially first kisses—are usually nervous, awkward, and over in the blink of an eye. So accidental first kisses should be even more forgettable, right?

Wrong.

His lips slide smoothly and sweetly over mine, and the taste of him makes every instinct in my body clamour, *yes, yes, yes!* It's like I'm seeing a new colour for the first time.

This would be about as easy to forget as being struck by lightning. Sort of feels the same way, actually.

Every single sensation is electrifying and sharp and new. The rough drag of day-old stubble against my cheek, the sharpness and angles of his body slamming into my chest, the low grunt of his voice, the warmth of his mouth, the firm grip of his fingers closing around both of my arms...

Shit.

At some point in all of these endless, dizzying moments, I'm pretty sure he stopped accidentally kissing me and started doing it on purpose.

I'm still too stunned to kiss him back... but I'm not *not* kissing him, either. It's just happening *to* me.

That's new, too. I've never been the one getting kissed like this: rough and raw, filled with a headstrong desire that drags an answer out from the depths of me.

Goddamn, it feels good.

I figured I'd come pick up this guy and my body would figure out right away that *he's a guy, and I'm a guy, and this won't work.* But it's exactly the opposite.

Now that I'm seeing my rescued castaway, breathing in his scent, touching him, *kissing* him...

It's not just my dick getting hard.

I mean, that's definitely happening—there's no denying the pleasant ache, the strain as my hard-on tries to fight its way out of my jeans, or the breathless tingle of arousal dancing across my skin.

But that same wildfire is melting something else inside me, too. Suddenly, it feels like I'm the one who's naked and flailing around, completely exposed to a stranger's scrutiny while I'm out of my depth.

I flinch, and just like that, it's over.

The stranger gulps a breath and lets go of me, grabbing the handrail instead. "Oh, shit."

I grunt and let go of him, grabbing the rope again with both hands.

All the better to keep myself from touching him again before I even know what I'm doing, what I want... or who I am.

"Oh my god I totally tripped, sorry—"

"No," I interrupt him firmly. "It's my fault, if anything. Jesus. *I'm* the one who should be sorry."

This is literally my job. I've never had a passenger trip like that before, and it should never have happened. The only thing stopping me from kicking myself nine ways from Sunday is the fact that it led to...

You know, that thing I can't think about yet.

The kiss.

"Wanna do me a huge favour? Don't tell my boss. Or, you know, sue us." I put all the good humour I can into my voice, so he'll know that I'm not mad at him. It's just that my world is still spinning around me.

The stranger's tiny, breathless laugh is squeaky with surprise—like an out-of-tune bell, but somehow charming.

"Deal?" I toss the rope onto the bow, turning to face him.

He nods as he carefully makes his way to the middle of the boat and sits on a cushioned bench. "We'll call it even if you give me that ride," he tells me with a mischievous little grin.

I straighten up and grin at him.

Just like that, I'm back on solid ground. The seas are calm, and the ferry is rocking so gently I barely notice it. My passenger and I are a *much* more professional distance apart. His wish is my command—the only limit is how much fuel I've got left in the tank.

"Of course," I promise. "Where can I take you?"

He doesn't even miss a beat. "As long as you ask my name, pretty much anywhere. I'll waive the dinner requirement."

I burst out laughing, shaking my head as I make my way to the cockpit of the tiny ferry. I'm going to do my best to ignore the innuendo, even if he doesn't make it easy.

At least he won't be boring.

"I'm Alph, and I'll be your skipper today. Er… tonight."

I turn toward him automatically, tapping my chest so he can see the name embroidered on my T-shirt. I certainly don't want him thinking I'm an Alfonso.

"Alph," Ronan repeats, his gaze flicking from my chest back up to my face as he smiles. "Cool. I'm Ronan, but I don't have it on a T-shirt," he startles another laugh from me with his good-natured ribbing. "And I left my ID at home, just in case I got busted for lewd acts in public."

His eyes sparkle with just enough mischief that I actually believe him, which makes it even funnier.

I don't think I've ever met someone as flamboyant or... as fun.

I lean against the inside wall of the cockpit, arms folded as I study him. "It's okay. Tonight isn't busy. We can skip the passenger manifest," I tell him with a wink. "Except for the destination."

Don't get me wrong, I don't want our conversation to be over. The only people I click with like this are my brothers—technically my best friends, but we're as good as family after growing up together on Sunrise.

And, let's be honest, it's not the same vibe at all. I definitely don't kiss *them*.

"Ah," Ronan murmurs.

Whoa.

It's like a clam snapped shut right in front of my eyes. Suddenly, the flirty, sassy, fun Ronan I've only just met is hiding away. He's back to the guy I found teetering on the edge of the dock like a stray, painfully wary yet desperate.

What did I say wrong?

Ronan pauses, and then he smiles—but this time, it feels like a wall going up.

Huh. Interesting.

Ronan folds his arms on the edge of the cockpit, peering innocently up at me. "Oh, Alph," he bats his lashes. "Is that your way of asking *your place or mine?*"

"I—I'm—where *is* your—" I break off, shaking my head. I barely understand the game we're in, but I'm about to play right into his hand. "Hold on. I'm not—I'm not trying to pick you up."

Ronan stifles a giggle as he looks around the ferry. "So far, I'd say you're doing a bad job, then."

I snort with amusement, reaching out as if to shove his arm before stopping myself.

The more I touch him, the harder it'll be to stick to my resolve.

I wave at him instead and fold my arms. "You know what I mean. And you should know that I've… well, I've always been straight."

Ronan's eyebrows creep up. The smirk finally disappears as he sits up to consider me, folding his hands in his lap. He's staring into my eyes in a way that makes me kind of squirmy, but not in a bad way.

And besides, I can't really look away.

Ronan shivers involuntarily, and it finally breaks the spell. "Shit," I groan. The poor guy must be freezing! "Let me get you a blanket." I stride to the storage bins under the rear benches.

Crouching there to rummage gives me a chance to calm myself down. My heart is racing at twenty knots a minute. That's no fit state to steer a ferry, much less explain a sexuality that suddenly feels like it's too slippery to be contained by a box I've never looked twice at.

"Gotcha."

I grab one of the light summer blankets and straighten up, unfolding him as I approach. I'm all ready to wrap it around his shoulders like I'm an emergency first responder.

Wait. Is that weird for a straight guy?

I stop in my tracks, the blanket draped awkwardly over my forearms as I catch Ronan's eyes. He tilts his head, but he doesn't say a word—not even a dirty joke.

Shit. He's not giving me an escape route.

He knows exactly what's happening, and he's waiting to see if I'll duke this out with myself… or turn tail and run.

To me, it isn't even a choice. I'm going to nip this shit in the bud.

I'm not the kind of guy who panics about what it means to touch another man. I've *never* worried about what a straight guy should or shouldn't do… and kissing Ronan isn't going to change that.

No matter how deliberate any part of it *might* have been.

I clench my jaw stubbornly as I lift the blanket like an offering.

Ronan inclines his head. He finally smiles at me, and I smile back. The tension eases again in my chest as I shake out the blanket, wrap it around him, and smooth it over his shoulders.

I sit right next to him, so close that our knees are touching, ignoring the gentle bump of the ferry's nose against the dock and the thickening, pleasurable crackle of tension between our bodies.

I'm not the only one trying to hide from something.

I catch Ronan's gaze, and then I ask the million-dollar question.

"Do you *want* to go home?"

CHAPTER

Four

RONAN

SHIT.

I don't even have the option of lying, swallowing my misery a little longer to figure things out on my own. That's what I would have done—before I made a promise to myself tonight.

Look after myself, even when that means asking for help.

Besides, the look on Alph's face tells me that he knew the answer to the question before he asked it.

"Um… no."

Alph nods. "Where *is* home?"

"A student apartment. Converted house, downtown. My roommates are…" I sigh, scratching the back of my head. I sound like an idiot if I describe all the shit they've pulled with me lately. "Assholes. They're the reason I'm stuck here."

Alph scowls so hard at the mainland that I can practically see a thundercloud forming over his head. "You were trying to get out for the night?"

"Yeah. But not… *out* out," I gesture all around us, at the great outdoors.

Alph nods slowly. He doesn't ask the inevitable questions, or—worse still—wrap me up in pity. He just smiles at me and puts a hand on my shoulder. "How about we get off this ferry and grab a drink?"

Oh.

That was the last thing I was expecting. Relief rushes through me, and I smile at him. "Yeah. Yeah, I'd like that. In town?"

"No can-do. But I know a good place."

"Is it yours?" I tilt my head, crossing my legs and rubbing my thighs. Just to keep them warm, of course.

"No," Alph grins. He gets up and heads to the ferry cockpit. "Well… it kind of is. But not really."

"What? Now you're talking in riddles." I squint at Alph. He just gives me a mysterious smile, so I roll my eyes. "Fine," I huff. "Keep your secrets."

He just grins at me. "You'll find out soon. Now, there's a catch."

"Yeah, there is." I smirk and rest my folded arms on one side of the three-sided plywood box surrounding the ferry cockpit. Then I make a point of looking Alph up and down.

Something tells me that I should push my luck and see what happens.

Alph gives me an amused sideways glance as he starts the engine. I wince, getting ready to cover my ears… but thank god, the rumble isn't *quite* as obnoxious as I expected.

"It's a little loud," Alph talks over the roar of the engine as the ferry starts moving. "I'm trying to convince my boss to go electric when we can't fix up this old gal anymore. He says a little noise is a good thing, and he doesn't want the passengers to hear the skippers fart." Alph solemnly shakes his head. "I keep telling him to cut down on the beans."

"Oh my god," I choke with laughter. Something is twinging in my side, but even clutching it while I laugh doesn't help.

Alph just cheerfully continues talking over the engine as he steers us for Sunrise Island. "So, here's the catch. If I've been drinking, I can't take the ferry home. That means you'll definitely be staying in my guest room."

Then he glances at me a couple more times, like he's trying to make sure I understand his meaning.

Oh. His guest room. He's trying to make sure I know that we're not going to share a bed.

Ugh. How respectful of him.

Alph isn't like the kind of guys I've chased before. He strikes me as the kind of man with principles. Someone who won't risk breaking someone's heart if he isn't sure he can be available for them.

I just want to climb him like a big, sexy, sturdy tree... but this tree has boundaries.

"Yeah," I say at last, raising my voice so he can hear me over the engine. "Thanks."

Alph gives me a quick glance and a smile, and his shoulders relax. "Phew. I was going to say, couches are available, if you'd prefer to suffer. Or floors."

"I have a comfortable bed fetish," I hastily reassure him. "Your guest room would be great, thanks."

Alph laughs, his eyes flicking across the dark water ahead of us. The islands are so close together that we're already at Sunrise Island, and he's glancing at his watch like he's calculating reefs and tides and stuff.

The headlight glances off a grimy, sea-worn old building that I'm pretty sure is actually floating over the water. Light and noise spills out of the open windows, along with the smell of freshly cooked food.

"Ohhh," I whisper. Alph's riddle suddenly makes sense. "Is *that* the place?" I ask.

"Yup," he beams, his barrel chest swelling with pride that makes me feel a little warmer toward the dingy exterior. "Sunrise's only floating restaurant, bar, and ferry terminal. Now hold on tight, and keep all arms and legs inside the vehicle."

Alph's smile is fading with concentration. He moves the throttle forward and back, fiddles with the wheel, and we start to drift sideways. We're close enough to the building that I'm worried we'll hit it.

Finally, I can't stop myself.

"What are you—"

Alph holds up a hand and grins at me. "Wait for it... almost..." I find myself holding my breath until he says, "*There.*"

Then he cuts the engine, pulls the keys out, and pockets them as the ass-end of the boat keeps swinging around. Within seconds, we've finished a full 180-degree turn to face the floating bar and the wharf next to it.

Alph whistles under his breath, strolling toward the bow like he has all the time in the world. Just as he picks up the rope, the ferry bumps into the wharf so gently and evenly that I could just step right off.

After my boarding experience, I won't... but I *could.*

Boys. I try to stifle my laughter, shaking my head as I stow my blanket and Alph ties her up.

"Shall we?" Alph asks, his eyes gleaming like he knows exactly what he did and he's waiting for me to say something.

I have to admit... it *was* pretty cool.

"Was that the boat equivalent of parallel-parking to impress a first date?"

Alph gives me a huge, boyish grin as he steps up onto the dock, then offers his hand. "Yes. Did it work?"

His excitement is so contagious that I can't help grinning back. "Actually, yeah," I admit, taking his hand for the step up.

My hand slides into Alph's large, strong palm. His fingers curl tightly, clasping me with a steady confidence that just distracts the *hell* out of me. My heart pounds against my ribcage, my knees trembling like jelly.

I step up onto the wharf, and then I stare up at Alph.

The skipper's breathing catches in his throat. His pupils go wide as he shifts and stands up straighter. The tip of his tongue darts out all of a sudden to moisten his lips.

I find my footing, but I keep on holding his hand and I count the seconds—two, three, *four* whole seconds—until at last, he thinks to let go and glances furtively at me.

Ha. Knew it.

One smug grin from me is enough to make Alph blush beet red as he turns to face the bar. "Right," he says and clears his throat. "Yep. Let's drop off the keys and see about that drink."

I stifle my laughter at his retreating back and follow in his footsteps. "Yeah, let's."

Who knows? Maybe tonight has a few more surprises up its sleeve.

CHAPTER
Five

RONAN

THE FIRST—AND MOST IMPORTANT—THING ABOUT SUNRISE'S floating restaurant/bar is the temperature.

Ahhhh. Nice and toasty.

Even with the windows open, the building seems to be clinging to the heat of a long August afternoon. It's almost enough to make me forget about freezing my ass off just minutes ago.

I pause just inside in the door, my eyebrows rising with surprise as I look around.

It's clean and bright in here, painted pastel yellow and blue—a far cry from the dingy dive bar I expected. In between the bar and restaurant is a glassed-in section, open to the sky and the water.

I think it makes us the main attraction for curious fish. But it's pretty damn cool.

"See? I know a good place, right?" Alph asks with a grin.

"You do. Even if it's the only place you know."

He laughs and leads me to the bar, nodding and smiling

to everyone who greets him while avoiding getting sucked into conversations.

I'm expecting to raise a few eyebrows, dressed like I am. But all I get are curious glances and welcoming smiles.

This is nothing like the Italian restaurant where we always go for our family dinners. It's the very definition of boring: for as long as I can remember, the same red candle has been in the same place on the same white tablecloth.

But this is a charming, pleasant chaos that makes me feel grounded. I can see why Alph wanted to bring me here. I can already tell a lot about the atmosphere on Sunrise Island, and it makes me wish I'd visited sooner.

"Kieran—" Alph breaks off, looking around for him. "Ah. Oh dear. The committee has him."

The bartender is a five-foot-something twink with a mop of pink hair and a bright smile on his face. He's surrounded by a gaggle of white-haired ladies, and he has a good-natured grin on his face.

"He's going to get flirted to death," Alph says with a laugh. Then he holds a finger to his lips.

What secrets am I about to learn? I lean in eagerly, and it's all I can do to focus on his words and not his warm breath against the side of my neck.

"My brother's on the committee. He hangs out with them a lot. Apparently they have this game of asking him the most in-depth questions just to listen to him talk." He straightens up and nods toward the bartender again, his eyes sparkling with amusement. "Look."

Kieran is wildly gesturing his hands as he explains something earnestly. The ladies are nodding along sweetly, but clearly not paying the slightest bit of attention to his words.

"Oh, my god. You're right." I cover my mouth to hide my laugh. "Should we throw him a life ring?"

"A life ring?" Alph gives me an amused look. "Look at you with the nautical metaphors. I'm rubbing off on you."

Rubbing off on me, huh? I don't even need to say it. All I do is widen my eyes innocently, then smirk at him.

Alph makes a little choking noise and pinches the bridge of his nose. "Oh, Ronan. At this rate, *you're* going to rub off on—" he realizes his mistake a little too late and trails off.

"Good. That means it's working," I tell him, batting my lashes as Alph gives me a pleasingly flabbergasted look. "Just… let me know if it's too much."

Alph scratches his neck, staring into the distance for a moment before he shakes his head. "That's not it. I'm just not used to having anyone run rings around me."

"Maybe it's good for you," I shrug.

Alph nods. "It is," he says without hesitation.

Whoa. I didn't expect him to take me seriously. I squint at him, but he's not sarcastic or joking around. He looks thoughtful, in fact, in a way that catches me off-guard.

I don't know what to say—and luckily, I don't have to say anything.

"Ah, you're back!" Kieran greets Alph, who tosses him the ferry keys. He catches them one-handed and hangs them on the wall, then folds his arms to look me over. "And *you're* the poor stranded laddie he went out to save."

He's a few inches shorter than me, with a strong Irish accent and a feisty grin. I relax and grin back at him.

"Yep. I'm *that* idiot."

Alph laughs softly and claps my shoulder. The pressure of his palm, even for a few moments, is… well, it takes an embarrassing amount of self-control not to gasp.

"Missed the last ferry?" The bartender sympathetically clicks his tongue against his teeth. "Must have given you a fright. You'll need a drink. What's your pleasure?"

Wait… does he mean for free?

I glance at Alph, who smiles at me. "It's your lucky night. Kieran never comps *me* drinks."

"Pfff," Kieran waves at him. "We'd go out of business if you got a free drink every time you parked the boat."

"*Docked* the boat," Alph corrects Kieran in a long-suffering groan.

Kieran nods. "Like I said. Parked the boat." Then he twitches a finger at me. "Come on, name it."

"Uh… vodka-soda? Thank you."

He winks at me and pirouettes to grab the vodka, flipping and spinning the bottle behind his back. "You were saying?" he asks Alph innocently.

I cough to hide my laugh as Alph scowls. It's nice to see him in his element with a friendly coworker. And it's even nicer to see that Alph doesn't give Kieran the same look he gives *me* for teasing him.

"A car gets parked. A boat gets moored," Alph continues. "I'll even accept *tied up*."

Kieran manages to keep a deadpan expression. "Scandalous. I learn something new about you every day." He glances meaningfully at me and winks, while I snort with laughter.

"Oh, I give up," Alph groans. He folds his arms on the bar top, gently thumping his forehead against them.

"There you are, gorgeous!" Kieran slides the finished drink to me. "Now… for the skipper whose… ahem… *mooring*… just deafened half my customers?"

Alph clears his throat sheepishly. "Oh. Uh. Just a beer on my tab, thanks."

Kieran cracks open a bottle, hands it over, and salutes us with one finger. "Enjoy. You'll be happy to know Berty's finished up for the night. Now, I'll distract your audience while you get away."

"What…" I trail off, watching him head back to the committee ladies.

They're stealthily glancing at me and Alph, and all of them are wearing mischievous grins.

Oh, god. I bet they know exactly what's going on.

I'm trying my hardest not to drape myself all over Alph, but I'm also not holding back from showing him how I feel. And I'm certainly not letting him off the hook for everything he wants.

It's so obvious that we feel the same magnetic pull. I just want to know why Alph is resisting it.

I glance around to check out the table situation before pointing at a table by the glass inner wall. "Let's sit there." It's the quietest spot, since most people are clustered around the open windows.

Alph sighs. "Are you sure? It's August," he mutters, glancing longingly at those windows as he tugs on the neck of his T-shirt.

"I, for one, am dressed for the conditions," I tell him with a hair toss before heading for the table.

When I glance over my shoulder, Alph is following. His deliciously kissable, sea-spray-salty lips are curved in a bemused smile that makes my belly flutter with nervous excitement.

I'm the one leading this dance, but we're twirling across

the wharf together, hand-in-hand. Plunging unstoppably toward the edge, and beyond it… a deep water that neither of us really knows.

It's time to sink or swim.

39

CHAPTER
Six

ALPH

I've never met someone quite like Ronan.

Fun, flirty, and wicked smart… that much is obvious. But he's also a walking enigma.

Ronan can be a high-energy chatterbox of endless dirty jokes, but when he wants to really make an impact, he can shut all of that off in an instant. He was calm, still, and almost *too* present as he watched me freak out about that stupid blanket.

Another example: he just strutted across the bar like he owns the place. And not even an hour ago, he was trembling on the edge of the dock like he thought I might not even see him.

Almost by accident, I've seen all these different sides of Ronan that seem like opposites at first… but as a collection, he makes sense.

He dazzles me, just by being himself.

That's the most baffling part of all. How could he think anyone would fail to notice him—and, more than that, *want* him?

I know I do.

But he's still not sleeping in my bed tonight.

Ronan's willing to respect that one line in the sand. He'll stand right on it, flirting outrageously. But I know I can't be swayed, so I don't mind it one bit. It's... it's actually really fun.

Those moments where Ronan is teasing me mercilessly, or looking me up and down like he's composing a to-do list... it drags out some new instinct in me. I find myself just wanting to shove him up against a wall and kiss him—this time, on purpose—and more.

So much more.

I'm aching to melt his triumphant grin into pure need, tease him until he's desperate, and then make him show me his unashamed ecstasy.

But... what if I give in, and then that's it? That's all he ever lets me have?

I'm already more interested in Ronan than I have been in anyone before. It's going to take a lot more than one night to figure out what that means for me.

"What should we toast?" Ronan asks me, picking up his glass as I slide onto the bar stool across from him.

I hum and tap my beer bottle on the table. Everything I can think of is way too romantic... or not romantic enough.

"To us?" I suggest at last.

He smiles and raises his glass to clink against my bottle. "To us."

We gulp a few sips of our drinks and settle down with contented sighs, measuring each other up now that we're finally face-to-face and alone in the light.

Holy crap. He's beautiful in a way that makes me stop and stare.

I can't help but appreciate the curve of his cheekbone and the soft swell to his lower lip. His eyebrows are arched like he's poised to make a sassy remark. His skin is smooth, except for the hint of stubble I felt earlier, along his jaw and upper lip.

But it's not just his physical beauty. It's the soft glow in his spirit that shines straight through his bright green eyes, drawing me in like a moth to flame.

"So," Ronan says, settling down and leaning slightly forward across the table. "How long have you lived here?"

"All my life—minus the last few years," I tell him. "I came back home this spring."

"Mm?" Ronan raises an eyebrow. "What's the story?"

"There isn't one, really. I moved to Alberta with my ex-girlfriend and got a job out there. It didn't work out."

"The job, or the ex-girlfriend?" Ronan gives a self-deprecating snort before he's even finished the question. "Sorry. That's a pretty dumb question."

"Both, actually," I smile wryly, waving off his sympathetic grimace. "We agreed to just be friends. I was working at the climbing gym nearby, so I figured I'd stay for a couple months. That became a couple years, until the gym closed and the ex wanted me to come work at her parents' ranch..."

I trail off and shrug as a flush of embarrassment creeps up the back of my neck. This is where the story usually stops, and people jump in to sympathise with me and scoff at the idea.

After all, nobody would be dumb enough to say yes, right?

But Ronan's figured it out already. He's watching me quietly, sipping his drink as he waits for me to go on.

"I said yes. They really needed a hand," I sigh. "But I didn't feel good about it."

"Oh?" Ronan murmurs. "How so?"

I scratch the back of my neck. "Helping them out made me happy at first. But little by little, they started to take advantage of my time, and so did my ex."

Ronan's eyes widen. "Oh, lord. Messy situationship? Did you get back together?" There's no judgment in his voice, just curiosity.

"God, no," I snort. "Kind of the opposite. She didn't care that I wasn't into her—to be honest, maybe I never was. But she wanted me to run the rest of her life anyway."

"Ouch," Ronan hisses, touching my hand across the table for a moment. "I'm sorry."

Suddenly, I feel dumb enough—or brave enough—to tell Ronan the part I've only told a few people, and never out loud.

"At one point she was like, *This is the kind of husband I want. A guy who'll do whatever I tell him to, and then leave me alone.* Like I was a robot vacuum or something." I huff a laugh, trying to lighten the mood.

Ronan's lips are slowly parting. His brows snap together as he stares at me. "What the hell? You're—you're not a robot."

"Don't worry. I didn't marry her," I force another laugh. "It was a good wakeup call. I came back home to help my brother get back on his feet, and then I got this job... and here I am."

Ronan smiles crookedly and holds up his glass for another toast. "To you being here tonight."

I laugh as I pick up my beer to clink against his glass, but

Ronan's watching me with a real sincerity that makes me stop and look at him again.

He doesn't just mean rescuing him from the beach.

That brand-new feeling is back.

My stomach flips with dizzying excitement. My heart is surging against my ribs like it wants to bust right out. Heat simmers along every inch of my skin, right down to the tips of my toes, until my pants feel tight again.

I know what this is—but only because I've never felt it like this before.

Desire.

Ronan's bright green gaze is still fixed on me. He smiles and holds up his glass again. "And to choosing ourselves."

I can't look away. Slowly, I raise my bottle and clink it against his glass again. "To choosing ourselves."

We both drink to that.

Ronan clears his throat. "I guess it's my turn now," he says, sliding his glass around the bar table with one fingertip.

Then, he shrinks in on himself, right here in front of my eyes.

Ronan's shoulders climb up, closer to his ears. He pulls his elbows in and tucks his knees together. His feet rest neatly on the bottom rail of the bar stool, and he even drags his glass a little bit closer to his chest.

Whatever the hell is going on, I don't like it.

The more Ronan furls up, the more I want to dive into whatever place he just went mentally and drag him out with my bare hands. But, as painful as it is, I know better.

Ronan has to move at his own speed. I promised myself when I moved back here that I'd never chase someone who isn't ready to be rescued. And when I say *ready*, I mean where

I found him today: teetering on the edge of the wharf, calculating how far and fast he can leap.

But is that where he's living with whatever this darkness is? I don't know yet. All I can do is stretch a hand out in the darkness... and pray that I'm not about to run aground.

CHAPTER
Seven

ALPH

"I'M IN MY LAST YEAR STUDYING FASHION DESIGN AT THE college," Ronan says.

Okay, that's not a bad start. It's pretty fucking cool. I've only seen Ronan in this one outfit, and I'm clueless about fashion, but I'm a little bit jealous that he's already found something he's obviously so good at.

I smile at Ronan, but he's staring at his glass, drawing tiny circles on the side with his fingertip.

"I was getting sick of the dorms, so I moved in with three of my classmates last year. Things were okay at first. But the grading got tougher and tougher, and… well…" His gaze is fixed on the glass, like he's embarrassed to even look at me. "They started doing better than me. The better they do—and the worse I do—the meaner they get."

Oh, shit. What a bunch of immature assholes.

"That's fucking *awful*," I tell him, gritting my teeth. "I'm so sorry you've had to live like that."

"I know." Ronan sighs. "I thought they'd chilled out over the summer, but they all just got back home, and…"

He clams up and stares at the table, so I reach over the table with my palm upturned to offer him strength. Ronan rests his fingers on mine, and then he finally sighs.

"Okay. You wanna know how I ended up on Maple Island? They figured out how to fake a location on Grindr and created a profile to catfish me. They told me to take the last ferry, and then… boom." He smiles crookedly. "*Surprise, guess who!*"

What the shit?

I stare at Ronan, my jaw hanging open. I'm so outraged that I can barely even form words.

Ronan peers at me. "Oh, Grindr's a dating app—"

Oh, god. I'm not *that* straight. "I know what Grindr is," I tell him, shaking my head. "That's not… I'm just… *why?*"

"I was stupid. I took the last ferry—" Ronan starts half-heartedly, and something inside me crystallizes into action.

I know what I can do for him.

"Nope." I set down my beer bottle loudly, and I crush his hand between both of mine. "No way. You're not going to do that to yourself, Ronan. Those assholes decided to screw you over. It's their fault."

A blush works its way up Ronan's cheeks as he stares at me, and I stare right back. I'm not letting him look away until I'm sure he's heard me.

"That's fucked up. Jesus, Ronan. You gotta find somewhere else to live."

Finally, Ronan's shoulders slump. He pulls his hand away and takes a deep breath. "Yeah, no. You're right. I can't afford to fuck up this semester. I have to move out."

"Yes," I breathe out with relief. "Get the fuck out of there."

Ronan nods, working his jaw around. "Classes start in a week. It'll be hard to find a place…"

That's it.

I know I'm grinning like the Cheshire Cat.

"My brother and I were sharing a house," I tell him. "I was in the apartment downstairs, and he was upstairs. But he's moved in with his boyfriend, so it's empty. I didn't want to rent it out to some random stranger…"

Ronan stares at me until he finally shakes his head. "So you thought you'd pick up a stranger on a beach?"

"Exactly," I grin at him, but I actually mean it. "If you can't trust a stranger on a beach, who *can* you trust?"

Ronan snorts. Then he does a double-take when he realizes I'm serious. "Dude. I-I know a *lot* of podcasts that would disagree with you. At least tell me you lock your doors."

"Uh… sometimes?" I laugh at the look on Ronan's face. "Hey, everyone who comes and goes has to get by me. Except the ones with their own boats, I guess."

Ronan sputters at me as I tip back my beer bottle and drain the last few drops.

Until these last few minutes, I didn't know exactly what ties together all these different sides of Ronan. Even when it disappeared, I couldn't put my finger on it. But now that the steady glow has returned to his eyes… it's impossible not to see it.

Hope.

"So, here's the plan," I tell Ronan when he's finished his drink. "You crash with me tonight, and as many nights as you want this week."

Ronan's jaw drops. He turns to look out the window toward the mainland, and it doesn't take a mindreader to know what he's thinking.

I don't have to go back there?

But I have one more thing to say, and it's important. I

don't want Ronan to feel committed to something he doesn't want, or that doesn't work well for him. After all he's been through, a perfect fit is the very least he deserves.

"Before we make any decisions, we'll see if you like the house—and the commute, and all the nuisances of living on an island. Either way, we'll figure it out," I tell him. "Sound good?"

Ronan swallows hard a few times and looks back at me. "Uh… yeah. It does." He sounds like he's in a daze. "It's… incredible." I reach out over the table to offer him a handshake, but Ronan grabs my hand in both of his. "Thank you, Alph. I just… I can't thank you enough."

"It's my pleasure," I promise. And it really is. The look on his face right now is reward enough. "So… you want to test out the walk home from the ferry?"

Ronan lets go of my hand and grins, bouncing to his feet. "Hell, yeah." Then he winks at me and puts a hand on his hip, turning side-on to me like he's beckoning me to come hither. "I thought you'd never ask."

"God," I laugh as we head to the door. "You're really made of rubber." I wave goodbye to Kieran, who winks at me, but I'm going to pointedly ignore that.

"What do you mean?" Ronan trots after me into the evening breeze.

"No matter how much you stretch, you bounce back to yourself in no time at all."

At first, I think the strangled noise is coming from the door closing. But then I turn a suspicious glance to Ronan, and he cracks up in a giggle.

Ohhh.

"Not *that* kind of stretch!" I groan and stride down the

wharf toward the firm ground of Sunrise Island, making Ronan trot to keep up with me.

"Hey, you're the one who said it." He's hot on my heels and breathless with laughter. "And you're not wrong. I'm *very* talented in the stretching department... among others..."

"I was—I didn't—"

I'm going to walk the whole way home with a boner if he keeps this up. And boy, is he good at keeping it up.

Great. Now he's got me doing it to myself.

I'm not going to win this one, so I throw my hands in the air to surrender. Ronan laughs, and I grin again, tipping my head back to breathe in that fresh, salty ocean air.

I'm glad Ronan's feeling like himself again... I just want to make sure he stays that way.

CHAPTER
Eight

RONAN

As we emerge from a wooded path to a gravel road, Alph grins and points at the first house we pass. "What's in the driveway?"

He's just spent the last few minutes insisting that the island only has one real car, and everyone drives golf carts. I was so convinced he was pulling my leg… but I can't deny my own eyes.

"It's a golf cart." I laugh at the smug grin on his face. "Okay, okay. I'm sorry I doubted you. Happy?"

"Yep." Alph beams at me. "You?"

My throat tightens. I can't explain how much lighter I feel, how much weight I've shrugged off since coming to Sunrise Island. I didn't realize what I've been carrying around with me… or for how long.

"Very," I tell him with a shiver.

Alph frowns with concern, crunching to a halt on the gravel road. "Here," he offers, raising his arm to make space next to him. "If you want to stay warm. It's always cooler here than on the mainland."

"Thank you." I scoot close to Alph before he can think twice. "Thank god I brought the hoodie, at least." He settles his arm around my shoulder, and I suddenly can't think straight.

The difference between us is about three inches of height and fifty pounds of muscle... and somehow, our bodies fit together perfectly. He's a furnace—and now that I'm thinking about his body, so am I.

"You really are my hero," I murmur.

He laughs it off and keeps walking, and I swallow hard.

Everything in me just wants to press closer to him, tilt my chin up to kiss him, take off *more* layers.

I want him to wrap me up in his arms, lift me off the ground, and surge inside me until we're sweating and moaning and panting each other's names...

God, this is killing me.

If I can tempt Alph to be less of a perfect gentleman, I won't cry about it. But it's actually really touching, too. I don't think anybody else has treated me with so much respect.

I doubt any of my Grindr guys would have saved me from *any* of this. Even if I sucked their dicks afterward... and I really do believe that Alph isn't trying to get anything out of me.

It's the weirdest thing. I already trust Alph so much. He's the kind of guy who'd give a stranger the shirt off his back. But he's really going above and beyond for me.

Why?

I should be more suspicious about him. I promised myself on Maple Island that I'd stop blindly relying on other people. Yet here I am, walking along a dark road and planning to live in a stranger's guest room.

"Penny for your thoughts?"

I snort. It would be kind of rude to tell him the whole truth, but… he did ask. "Just hoping I'm not going to end up on a podcast any time soon."

Before I can clarify, Alph lights up and squeezes me even tighter around the shoulders. "Oh! You'd be great on a podcast, though. Like, talking about your clothes…?"

Oh, my god.

My heart melts at his adorably clueless grin. He's being so supportive and sweet that I can't actually bring myself to tell him I listen to true crime podcasts.

I bet he doesn't even know what they are. It seems like a genre that would only give him more things to worry about.

"Yes, sweetie," I laugh, looking up at the star-covered sky. "To talk about my clothes."

I glance back down, and Alph is watching me with that look on his face again… like he's totally bemused, yet fascinated.

A thousand butterflies in my stomach launch into flight at once.

It sounds silly, but honestly, the way he looks at me makes me feel a little bit faint. The silence is suddenly straining under the tension between us. Nestled into his side, something draws me toward him. I'm fighting this chemistry with all my might.

Don't kiss him again. Don't kiss him again. I can't fuck this up by kissing him again…

"I'm basically a stranger, you know," I blurt out. "Staying in your home. How come you trust me so much? What if… what if I rob you blind?"

"Then what?" Alph smiles. "It's an island."

He's got a point.

"Then I steal a boat…"

"And the keys?" Alph is obviously trying not to grin.

"A rowboat," I insist, my cheeks flushing. Alph is barely holding in his laughter, and I'm a tiny bit insulted. "I can steal a rowboat and row to the mainland."

"We'll ignore the question of how you get all my valuables *to* the rowboat," Alph says, his eyes sparkling with amusement. "Do you know how to row?"

"Fuck."

I'd definitely end up on the news for getting washed out to the Pacific Ocean while clutching a sixty-inch TV. Alph's right. I'm not cut out to be a criminal mastermind.

But that still doesn't explain why I find it hard to trust even the fact that *he* trusts *me*.

"Stick around and I'll teach you."

"…To steal TVs?" The words come out of my mouth before I slap my forehead. "Oh, duh. To row."

Alph stops walking and doubles over with laughter as I blush to my toes. But I won't lie: it's worth making an ass of myself to hear that belly laugh.

"Yeah," he finally manages, and then he clears his throat. "I mean, if you like this place, of course. I don't want to pressure you."

"Mmm." I pretend to give him a suspicious look. "You don't live in a horror house, do you?"

Alph looks genuinely worried, like he thinks I might actually believe that. He squeezes my shoulder hastily. "No. God, no. It's not huge, but I keep it up well—"

"Alph!" I laugh. "I'm teasing."

"…Oh." He snorts and rubs his neck sheepishly. "But it's not just the house. It's island life. Don't get me wrong, there's nowhere like Sunrise, but it's a lot to get used to."

Too late. I've already decided that I love this place.

I've never had such a pretty, moonlit walk home. We're surrounded by trees, and I can hear the ocean in the distance. We've been passing all kinds of houses: romantic cabins with tiny gardens, big glass mansions tucked away at the back of their lots, and everything in between. An eclectic mix, just like the locals at the bar.

I guess you have to be a little bit weird to want to live on an island, and I've got more than enough weirdness to qualify.

It's an artist's dream.

"I mean, I'll see how I feel in the morning," I shrug. "But I think this is exactly what I need. If I'm going to have any chance of pulling this off... I need all the creative inspiration I can get."

Alph swivels his head to blink owlishly at me. "Pulling what off?"

Great. *Now* I remember that I told him about my room-mates... but not the ultimatum.

"Okay," I sigh. "Just promise you won't judge me."

Alph squeezes me around the shoulders. "I promise."

Damn it... I believe him.

CHAPTER
Nine

RONAN

ALL WEEK, I'VE BEEN SIMMERING WITH GUILT—AND MORE than a little shame.

It's hard to look at Alph while I talk. I remember the look of admiration he gave me at the bar when I told him about my degree, and… I don't want to see it in his face, if I lose his respect now.

"It's the final year of my degree. This semester, we're developing our first solo mini-collections. There's a runway showcase in December to decide who gets the best work experience placements. I could end up sweeping floors… or I could work for XX Gracieux," I sigh dreamily.

Alph smiles at me. "There's a reason Sunrise has lots of artists. You'll find all the inspiration you need here. You're going to be top of the class, I just know it."

My stomach lurches. Alph's smile is only making things worse, because I don't feel like I deserve his confidence in me.

"Before you say that…"

"Hm?"

I sigh. "So… I'm the youngest of three boys. Our parents are accountants who started their own firm. They paid for us all to go to school. My brothers studied accounting, and now they're working at the family business."

Alph whistles under his breath. "Jesus. Your family must live and breathe spreadsheets."

I crack up, because it's true. "You have no idea. Road trips, ball games, Tooth Fairy visits… everything has to make sense to the database." Ouch. My smile fades as I sneak a look up at him. "And… that's kind of the problem."

Alph is watching me with a look of understanding. He nods, his arm tightening around my shoulders. "You don't fit into a database, and that's okay."

"Yeah. But it's more than that. They didn't mind me studying fashion design. But…" My gut twists in knots. "Remember I said my grades were getting bad? They gave me an ultimatum this week. If the showcase doesn't go well…"

I can't bring myself to say it. I grimace, making a chopping motion with one hand.

Alph comes to a halt, his arm still around my shoulders as he raises his eyebrow. "Beheading? That's awfully medieval."

It's so unexpected—and hilarious—that I burst out laughing until I'm almost crying, clinging to Alph's shoulder to stay upright.

"Sorry," Alph says, dropping his arm from my shoulders as we set off again. "It's serious, I know."

"Don't be sorry. Thank you." Another giggle slips out as I shake my head. After spending a week feeling like shit, I can't believe he's found a way to make me laugh about it.

Everything feels a little more manageable now.

Alph mentioned he had a brother, didn't he? He must be the big brother. It's something my brothers would do…

except Alph manages to be funny, whereas Garrett and Reid just try their hardest to annoy me.

"You were saying?" Alph asks.

"Basically, if I don't pull my grades up this term, they won't pay for my final term. Three years down the drain."

"That's stressful. But, look. You're not in the same place you were last year, right?"

I chew my lip around. Will that be enough?

"You're going to do fine," Alph tells me with so much confidence that I just about believe him. "One thing at at a time. Speaking of which..." he gestures toward the house coming up on our left. "This is it."

"Ohhh," I breathe out with a grin. "That's so cute! Not at all a horror house."

Alph huffs with laughter as he opens the little white front gate and holds it for me. "Thank you, I think."

We walk up the path toward the small family home, painted a bright cornflower blue. The front yard is full of neatly tended flowerbeds and a little patch of lawn.

"Come on up. This half would be yours," Alph says as he reaches the front steps of the porch. He points to the stepping stone path that winds around the side of the house. "I'm in the apartment downstairs. The entrance is in the back."

"Famously," I murmur with a wicked grin.

Alph's totally trying to pretend he didn't hear me, but he can't stop the amused snort as I trot up the stairs after him.

He pushes open the front door without even unlocking it, and I swallow back my lecture for now.

I just can't believe this might be mine.

Alph flicks on the landing light, and as I step inside, I gasp.

The staircase walls are painted a beautiful sage green. The

wall leading upstairs has been turned into a huge gallery wall, with an eclectic mix of family photos and artwork in different frames.

"Do you like it?" Alph asks, watching me anxiously. "I only just did it last month. I'm not sure about those smaller frames. It might look cluttered…?"

"It's perfect," I promise. I'm not going to tell Alph that I'm already planning to sneak down here in the morning for more clues about who he is. "This was your family home growing up?"

Alph's chest swells with pride. "Thanks. Yeah, it was." He bends over to unlace his shoes. "I'm trying to update it without losing the important things."

"So far, so good." I sink onto the bottom step to take my shoes off. "I can't wait to see the rest."

Alph flicks on the other light switch, heading upstairs as I follow him. Then he turns to me and beams with earnest pride, flourishing both hands to indicate everything around us.

Hardwood floors, an open-plan living room with a cast-iron fireplace, a kitchen through the nearest doorway, and a hallway that must lead to the bedrooms…

It's *beautiful*.

I finally tear my gaze away from our surroundings to look at Alph again. He's watching me for my reaction, and whatever he sees in my face makes him grin.

"Welcome home."

I think I might just die.

"Okay. That's everything, I think," Alph declares, following me to the guest room. "I'll bring some things up from my place. Towels, PJs for you, snacks..." he ticks off on his fingers. "Are you hungry?"

I sink onto the guest room bed with a blissful sigh. "Um... am I?" I think I'm too exhausted to decide.

Alph's smile softens. "You must be tired. If you want a shower, it's the door across the hall. I'll leave everything outside your door. Except the snacks, of course." He laughs. "They'll be in the fridge. Or on the counter, depending on the snack."

Until now, Alph has been so calm that it's cute to see him getting so excited. I don't think he has guests very often.

Or else there's some other reason he's excited to have me in his house... and I'd prefer to think it's the latter.

"Thank you," I laugh.

Alph nods. "If you need anything, I'll stay upstairs tonight. I'm in the in the room at the end of the hall. We can sleep in tomorrow—my shift doesn't start until lunchtime."

I groan with relief. "I was worried I might have to be up at dawn."

"Not at all," Alph grins. "If you come with me to work, I can give you a ride to town and back... but only if you want."

I gulp at the thought of going back there... even to move out.

"Wait until the morning to make up your mind," Alph says, and I flinch at the sympathy written all over his face. "You can get a ride anytime."

I clear my throat. "*Two* rides in one day? I'll definitely have to find a way of repaying you."

"I'm not asking for—" Alph breaks off his sentence when

he notices my smirk. "*Ferry* rides," he adds with a roll of his eyes, blushing fiercely.

He's thought about it, too.

"If you like," I tell him, batting my lashes innocently. I fold my hands in my lap, one on top of the other. "I prefer to be called other names."

Alph's lips slowly part, and then he pinches the bridge of his nose with one hand as he steps back from the doorway. "Good night, Ronan."

"Good night!" I giggle as he slowly closes the door on me. His footsteps head down the hall and down the stairs, and then…

I'm alone.

It's so peaceful that I barely know what to do. I take a deep breath and then another, wriggling against the fluffy white comforter as I look around.

The pale lilac curtains are closed, but I'm pretty sure the window overlooks the backyard. In the corner is a closet with wooden folding doors that look like they're originals, but gleam like they're new.

"What time is it, anyway?" I finally dig my phone out of my pocket, and when I press the power button, it won't turn on. No surprise, after the day I've had.

The alarm clock on the bedside table says it's after one in the morning, and I see another cable on the table, too. Knowing Alph, I'd better get up to try it.

Yep. My phone plugs in perfectly. This guy is an actual saviour.

Since I'm already standing, I flick the lights off and head to the window, tugging open the curtains. I slide the window open, too, and then fold my arms on the windowsill to lean there and look out.

My eyes are slowly adjusting to the darkness. The whole walk home feels like a dream that's coming back to me: trees, the faint sound of the ocean, and the August breeze that's surprisingly pleasant now that I'm inside.

"Fuck," I breathe out. "This place is perfect."

Not just to run away from a shitty situation… but to run towards my future.

Maybe it's my exhaustion and the late hour, but it feels like my life is suddenly full of possibilities. I can't imagine what a semester here would do for me—or even a whole year.

But there's one teeny-tiny complication: I'm coming here to work my ass off to rescue myself.

I can't afford distractions. But I can't see how *not* to be distracted by Alph. He's six-foot-something of pure, muscled, earnest, lighthearted, stupidly crushable distraction.

"God," I breathe out, tugging the curtains closed as I flop onto the bed. "What am I going to do?"

CHAPTER

Ten

ALPH

My phone is buzzing insistently on the nightstand. I grope around until I find it, poking at the screen, but it's not my alarm or an incoming call.

Must be notifications. Damn it. I hate when that happens.

"Shush, you," I groan, and my phone actually seems to listen. It buzzes once more and then goes still.

I crack my eyes open to figure out where I am, and then I smile sleepily and roll over in bed to admire the gleaming hardwood floors.

It's funny how this has never been *my* bedroom but I've renovated it top to bottom, twice. The first was after my parents moved out, and then after my little brother moved out to live with my best friend—his boyfriend, Carter. All my hard work was worth it, though.

Sanding, cleaning, painting… everything but screwing, so to speak.

Shit. I sit bolt upright. *What's that noise?*

The shower's running. I'm not alone… and it's all flooding back to me.

"Ronan," I breathe out.

What a night.

The dramatic Maple Island rescue, drinks at the bar, the walk home…

I can't help glancing to the other side of the bedroom, just in case my memory is failing me… but there's not even an imprint on the pillow.

Right. Yes. We didn't sleep together. Of course.

Telling myself that doesn't erase the insistent memory of the soft, sweet warmth of Ronan's lips on mine. My body can't forget his willowy body shivering as he presses against me, seeking my heat, and my…

Whoa, there.

Now I'm awake… and hard as hell. Maybe I'll sneak downstairs to my own apartment. I need a long, hot shower somewhere I won't be disturbed…

"Dude, I thought you were dead!" A voice echoes in the hallway. "Ever heard of checking your damn phone?"

"Oh, shit."

That's not Ronan. It's Carter, and his voice is getting louder, like he's stomping toward the bedroom to ream me out… or the bathroom.

My best friend and I used to be in gym class together. He wouldn't think anything of sticking his head in the bathroom to trade friendly insults. Meaning he's about to scare the ever-loving shit out of my…

I don't know what to call Ronan, but that's not the priority right now.

"Shit, shit, shit…!"

I've never moved so fast in my life. Almost before I tumble out of bed, I'm grabbing my bathrobe and shoving it on, tying it closed, reaching for the doorknob—

I burst out into the hall, skidding to a halt on the gleaming hardwood floor.

"Carter! Hold up!"

"Huh?" Carter lets go of the bathroom doorknob just as the shower water turns off. His confused squint turns to the bathroom door, and back to me. "*Huh?!*"

My friends have never known me to bring someone home like this. Or like he's assuming I have, anyway. The exact details are kind of irrelevant. It's easy to tell what conclusions he's about to jump to. "I don't—I'll explain, just—"

Ronan's voice echoes in the bathroom. "What—in fuck's name—is going on out there?"

He punctuates the question by yanking the door open. Steam billows out, and there he is, standing in the doorway.

I freeze like a deer in the headlights.

However hard I try to fix my eyes on his face, I can't help following the trickle of water droplets from his soaked hair, down his smooth chest, straight to the towel wrapped around his waist.

Nope. Not looking. Not looking. Stop looking. Seriously.

Ronan's staring at me, too. His brows are furrowed, his cheeks flushed as he slowly looks me from top to bottom. All I can do is pray that my bathrobe is thick enough to do the job.

Thick enough to... oh, my god. He really has rubbed off on me.

Carter's the first one to come to his wits. "Shit. Oh, shit. G-Guys," he stumbles over himself, glancing at Ronan quickly again, "I'm sorry. Uh... I didn't know you had—"

"I picked him up last night—"

"*Phrasing,*" Ronan murmurs under his breath. I can't tell if his voice is strained with amusement or annoyance.

I blush all the harder and slap my hand on my forehead. "Fuck." I wish the floor would open up and swallow me whole, but I've fixed and polished it up too carefully.

Carter strides down the hallway like he's been stung by a wasp. "Dude, it's so cool. We'll talk later," he says, waving over his shoulder at Ronan. "Uh... sorry again... good to meet you... bye!"

I cast Ronan my most apologetic stare, but he doesn't seem mad. Nor is he in a hurry to preserve his modesty. He just smirks and folds his arms, leaning in the doorway. "Don't let me get in the way."

If I keep looking at Ronan, this situation will get even more awkward, real fast. But I can't shake the overwhelming desire to stare at the expanse of bare skin. My belly is prickling with heat, and I'm getting a little lightheaded...

I rush after Carter just as he reaches the stairs. "Hold on, man. It's fine. It's just a long story. Look, meet me downstairs in a minute, yeah?"

Carter pauses and peers over his shoulder with surprise, one hand on the top banister. "You're sure?"

"I'll make coffee—" I cut myself off with a groan.

Shit. That's it.

I was supposed to meet him for coffee this morning, and I totally blew him off. That never happens. No wonder he came busting in like he was ready to give me first aid.

"Dude, I get it." Carter laughs at the look on my face. "It's fine. You have a good excuse."

I scowl at him, because it's not. I don't forget appointments, and I *don't* let people down. Whenever I do, I feel like shit.

"As long as you're not dead, just busy..." Carter's lips twitch as he raises an eyebrow at me. "Everyone sleeps in sometimes. I know you're Mr. Responsible, but stop beating yourself up about it."

He's being a lot nicer than he could be, considering how mad I got about him dating my little brother when he realized he wasn't straight.

Actually, he's the perfect person to talk to right now.

"He's right," Ronan calls out from the bathroom door. "You were up really late last night being Mr. Responsible."

Carter looks like he's about to crack a rib from trying not to laugh.

"Ronan…" I sigh, raising my eyes to the ceiling.

"Ronan?" Carter smirks.

"Nice to meet you!" Ronan calls. "It was Carter, right?"

"You got it. Hey, you wanna join us for coffee?" Carter asks Ronan as my eyes widen. "And donuts. But I only brought half a dozen, and I want two, so…" He counts on his fingers. "We're fine, as long as there's no more than three of you."

Ronan's laugh rings through the hallway like music, but I still glare daggers at my best friend. "I'm going to kill you," I mutter under my breath, and he just grins mercilessly.

"Sure!" Ronan yells, closing the bathroom door. "I just need a few minutes… and some respectable clothes." Then the shower turns back on.

Carter opens his mouth for another smart-ass remark, but I jab my finger toward the bottom of the staircase, and the internal door to my unit. "Door's unlocked."

It's the nicest possible way of telling him to get out.

"All right, all right." Carter saunters down the stairs, still grinning his ass off. "I'll start the coffee. Sounds like we've got a lot to catch up on."

He disappears through the door and I groan, running my hands through my hair.

At least one of my new problems has an easy answer: my little brother left some of his clothes here when he moved in with Carter. He's about the same size as Ronan, I think. I pause by the bathroom door for just long enough to call out, "Try on the clothes in your dresser. They oughta fit." He makes some sound of acknowledgment, and I flee for the master bedroom.

The moment the door is closed, I loosen the tie on my bathrobe and collapse face-first onto the bed. My phone is vibrating on the bedside table again, and now I recognize the pattern. It means there's a notification in my group chat with all my best friends.

Including, of course, Carter. *God knows what he's saying.* My face still buried in the comforter, I flip my phone the bird and groan.

At least today can only go up from here.

CHAPTER
Eleven

ALPH

I skim the last few messages in the group chat as I walk down the stairs to my apartment. Most of the 43 new notifications are from Carter.

CARTER

Alph???

bro

answer the door dude

wtf….. you're not here? are you upstairs or dead???

okay if you don't read these messages in 60 seconds i'm coming upstairs

Then the time stamps jump forward to a couple of minutes ago.

CARTER

update: he's alive, ignore everything above

extremely my bad bro

i can head home if you wanna catch up later

just let me know

MURPH

???

DREW

WTF is happening?

CARTER

he slept in

ZACH

There's a story, and we want it.

CARTER

ok so he was up late

...and slept in

now go the fuck to sleep

MURPH

Don't quit your day job to become a children's author.

ZACH

Nice try, Carter. Islands have no secrets.
Spill...

Carter hasn't responded again, but I know my friends. This is only going to get worse until I say something.

I pause by the door to tap out a few quick messages.

You're all a bunch of busybodies. Thanks for trying, Carter.

Everything's fine but it was a hell of a night.

I'll fill you all in ASAP.

There. That'll tide them over until *I* figure out what the hell's going on.

I heard the shower turn off just when I finished getting dressed, so I don't think we have long before Ronan joins us. And there's some stuff I should probably fill Carter in on first.

The smell of coffee greets me as I tuck my phone away and push open the basement door.

Thank god for that. Everything makes more sense with a cup of coffee in hand.

Carter's sprawled in one of the dining chairs, looking at his phone. Probably reading my messages. The sliding doors to the back deck are open, letting in the fresh air and sunlight.

"So," I say to announce myself as I head for my kitchen to grab a mug and the coffee pot.

Carter turns to grin at me, setting his phone down. "So. Sounds like a hell of a story. Gonna tell me everything?"

I hesitate. This is the part I hadn't really planned, because every time I tried to rehearse it in my head, something different came out.

I accidentally kissed this guy, Ronan, and he might be my roommate—I mean, tenant. What the fuck do I do now?

I saved Ronan from a beach and he's moving in... but I swear we haven't had sex yet. I mean, ever. I mean, not that I wouldn't.

I've never met someone like him and he needs a place to rent, and I'm really hoping he likes me—I mean, me and the island and the house...

Yeah, no. I steady my hands on the coffee pot to pour a mug full, then set it down to grab the cream. "Where the fuck do I start?"

"The beginning?"

"Smartass." I lean on the counter, clutching a little teaspoon for dear life. "Fine. So I rescued him from Maple Island last night. We got a drink at the bar. Turns out he's living with shitty roommates, and he needs to move out. And pull up his grades in fashion school by the end of the year, or his parents won't pay for his last semester."

I plop down into the chair opposite Carter, but he isn't saying a word. He just stretches his legs out over the sill of the sliding door, props one ankle over the other, and turns his head to me.

As I struggle for words, Carter just waits.

At last, I give him a helpless shrug. "I don't know, man." I raise my mug to blow on the surface of my coffee. "I don't know."

That's not quite true. I *do* know, somewhere in my gut... but I can't define it. Not that I care about definitions, but I do care about expectations: Ronan's, my own, and everyone else's.

I don't want to set anyone up for disappointment.

Carter raises his eyebrows and whistles. "Wow. You've got it bad."

"I..."

That nervous excitement is back, vibrating through my bones with giddiness about being named and recognized. I know Carter is right, but the rest of me wants to fight it. I want to say it's impossible, that I barely know him. I can't possibly explain the way my world tipped on its axis the moment I saw him.

"I think so," I admit.

Truth is, I *know* so. Ronan feels inevitable. Not in a bad way, but in a *big* way that I wasn't ready for.

I turn to watch the birds come and go from the feeder. It's

already mostly empty. I'd better fill it up today, or the wood-peckers will start hammering on Ronan's window at dawn.

"Huh." Carter tilts his head. "I've never seen you like this. You've had, what, a couple girlfriends? Three, right?"

"Technically. I'm not sure the first two count."

Both times, it didn't even last a month, so I promised myself I'd choose right the third time. Which is how I ended up in Alberta, teaching myself plumbing from Youtube at midnight because my ex's parents' pipes were frozen.

"Whatever," Carter waves off the details. "Point is, it always felt like… well." He sips his coffee hastily, pausing like he isn't sure I'll like the next part.

"What?" I look over at him. "Hit me with it, man."

We don't pull punches with each other. That's not what best friends do.

"Like you were checking off a to-do list." Carter puts down his mug to raise his hands, miming a notepad and pen, ticking off items. *Get girlfriend, find a nice 9-to-5, fix up house, have two kids…*"

I bristle and frown at him. I know I asked for it, but I don't like his tone. "What's wrong with wanting that stuff?"

Carter rolls his eyes. "Cool it," he tells me. "Nothing. But you've never talked about *wanting* them. The girlfriends or the rest of it."

Oh.

Now that he's gotten to the point, my annoyance is simmering down. I guess he's right. I don't know if I want all those things. But I do want what they mean to me: a sense of direction and purpose. Knowing what I'm supposed to be doing, what rules to follow. What comes next.

For a long time now, I've felt like I'm doing the right things but I'm still lost at sea.

"I figured that's how it's works," I tell him with a shrug. "You pick someone, you commit real hard, and you settle down…"

"Uh huh," Carter says. "Now imagine all that, but if you gave a fuck."

"Excuse me?" My eyebrows climb, right along with my temper. I might have hurt people before from not knowing what I wanted, but that doesn't mean I didn't *try*, damn it. I set down my mug hard. "I always give a fuck—"

"Bite my head off in a minute if you want," Carter tells me calmly, not taking the bait. "I'm gonna go out on a limb here and say something. I bet it's easier to be Mr. Responsible if you don't want anything for yourself."

My jaw drops.

I'm glad Carter isn't pulling his punches. But sweet Jesus. It feels like I've been steering blindly through the fog, and I just found land… the hard way.

"Am I right?" Carter asks. And to his credit, he isn't even smug. He's watching me with a frown that tells me he's been worried about me for a while.

"Dude," I finally manage. "*Dude.*"

"Yeah, bro." Carter relaxes and grins at me. "So I think this guy's gonna scare the crap out of you, and it'll be good for you."

I stare at him, palms slowly roasting around my coffee mug. "Yeah?"

"Ohhh, yeah." Carter looks way too pleased with himself, raising his coffee again. "Man. I finally see why the managers get off on the post-game debrief. It's way more fun when you weren't on the ice."

When I flip him off, he laughs, and then I finally manage a grin back at him. Then I lean in across the table, suddenly excited. I wish I could figure out how to tell him everything, because I know he'll get it.

"I don't know how to explain it. It happened so fast. I saw him, and I just…" I trail off, staring into the distance. Something in me feels different than it did yesterday morning, all bright and eager and excited.

But that sounds stupid to say out loud.

Carter laughs. "You two do anything yet? Please tell me yes."

"Uh…" I don't think he means an accidental kiss, even if it rocked my world. "No…?"

Carter grunts. "Let me guess. You're not sure what you want, and you're trying not to break his heart. Been there, done that." He smiles wryly at me. "Nearly fucked it up. Trust me. Take a chill pill and mess around. Explore. Doesn't mean you have to walk down the aisle… unless you want to."

Wait a minute. He's got this little smile on his face all of a sudden.

Holy shit. Is this his way of telling me he's going to propose to my little brother?

"Do *you* want to?"

"Nuh uh uh. Don't try that," Carter folds his arms. "This isn't about me. It's about you finally thinking about what makes you happy… even if it's not what makes Ronan happy. Or me, for that matter. Or anyone else."

Well, *there's* a scary thought.

Before I can cuss him out, footsteps patter down the stairs at top speed.

Ronan's coming.

My heart rate instantly picks up, and I catch my breath as I sit upright and turn to face the door. He's not even in the room yet, but I'm dizzy with anticipation.

And isn't that just a fancy word for wanting?

The door bursts open, and Ronan flies through it.

He's dressed in an old, faded black T-shirt, and the ripped jeans Felix wore to help repair the family boat. No wonder my brother left them behind... but on Ronan, they look *cool*.

Come to think of it, I can't imagine anything that wouldn't look cool on him.

"Whoa," Ronan yelps, skidding to a halt. He looks around, spots us watching him, and blushes. "I really underestimated gravity."

I burst out laughing as I get to my feet. "I used to do that as a kid, but the door wasn't there. Please don't break your nose."

"Seconded. It's no fun," Carter says.

Ronan giggles. "Noted. Am I too late for donuts?"

"Wait a minute, wait a minute. Am *I* too late?" I turn to Carter.

He's pulling a donut box out from a bag under the table. "No. I didn't want you to eat them all before Ronan showed up."

"That's very nice of you," Ronan beams at him as he bounces toward us.

Just seeing him so happy makes *me* happy—and fills me up with restless energy. I stand up quickly. "I'll get you a coffee."

"Thanks!"

"Did you sleep all right?" Carter asks. I can tell he's dying to figure out what kind of guy caught my eye after all this time.

"Like a rock," Ronan says, grabbing a donut and pulling it in half. "Mind you, I probably could have slept on the beach after all, I was so tired."

Carter laughs. "I'm glad you didn't. I heard it was a rough time."

"You have no idea." Ronan launches into the whole story with gusto, surprising even me.

As I pour coffee—and wait for the chance to ask about milk and sugar and cream—I can't help but grin. It doesn't surprise me that Carter and Ronan are already getting on like a house on fire, but Carter's the one who says it first.

"Man, you ought to meet Flick," he tells Ronan as I slide him the coffee and sit down again. "Felix, that is. My boyfriend, his little brother."

"Whose clothes you're wearing," I add. "But you look better in them."

Ronan beams at me in a way that makes me feel like there's sunshine pouring straight into my soul.

"No offence, Ronan, but I'm legally obligated to disagree," Carter says.

Ronan laughs. "It's okay. This is too conservative for me anyway. I need cutouts." I don't know what that means, and obviously Carter doesn't either, because Ronan snorts. "Oh, lord. Fine. When I bring my portfolio here, you'll see."

I freeze, coffee mug halfway to my lips.

When. He said when, not if.

"Oh yeah?" Carter says. "Alph said you were thinking about moving in."

I owe him a case of beer for how cool he's being right now, because I am decidedly *not*.

"Thinking about it?" Ronan giggles, shaking his head as he looks at me. "My mind's made up, honey. Give me a lease and I'll sign it today."

My hands curl even tighter around the mug as I stare at him.

He's moving in. This guy I can't stop wanting... he's going to be living with me. Or just above me, but that's basically with me.

"G-Great!"

Great? Seriously? That's all I can come up with?

Carter pumps his fist in the air. "Yeah! New neighbour. Hi, new neighbour." He reaches out to high-five Ronan, who laughs and returns the high-five. Then he whips out his phone. "Let's iron it out right now."

Details. Yes. Thank god.

If we have details to iron out, maybe I can stop thinking about what it would be like to kiss Ronan every night...

Oh, who am I kidding?

It's all I can think about now.

CHAPTER
Twelve

RONAN

It's moving day, and my roommates don't even know.

Not that they care. After three nights away from home, none of them have so much as messaged me to check if I'm still alive. They're either feeling so guilty they can't acknowledge me or they're coldblooded motherfuckers who want to maintain plausible deniability.

I know how far they'll go for petty revenge. So I waited until they're all at their studio for their weekly strategy meeting—whatever that means—and then came home to pack up for good.

Soon, I'll be free.

Free to make a new home, a new future... and to figure out how Alph is going to fit in.

Mmmm. I hope he stretches me in ways I've never felt before...

"Packing," I mutter desperately, flapping a hand in front of my face to cool off. "Packing first."

Alph is on the way to his boat with most of my stuff. He'll be back soon for me and the last few suitcases. I shove the last shampoo bottle into the corner of the suitcase and flip it shut, then plop my ass on top to help force the zipper up.

Not daydreaming about him is a losing battle, but at least I can keep my hands busy. And *if* I finish packing before he gets back… I can keep my hands busy some other way.

Just like that, I'm packing again at top speed.

The pile of clothes on the floor is almost gone, and there's just one more hanger.

"Ugh," I flinch as I pick it up. "That's a boner-killer."

This is the one shirt I've been dreading seeing ever again. My final project last year, shoved in the back of the closet since April… but I can't avoid it any longer.

Seeing it now is like a fever dream that brings everything flooding back.

We only had 24 hours, start to finish and I barely slept.

The first thing I did was ask my brothers for old dress shirts. They teased me for asking, instead of just stealing and "improving" them like I did when I was a kid. But, as it turned out, they had almost identical shirts to give me: one black and one white.

I knew I was onto a winning idea.

I ripped the shirts apart at every seam, cut a continuous strip of blood-red lace and carefully added it between every single piece. Then I reassembled it all to make one shirt. It was hell making sure there were no ragged seams, but I was determined not to make it a DIY punk statement.

My roommates seemed to take it in turns to bug me, constantly interrupting me for pointless reasons while I was sewing. But I stuck with it, because I wanted to prove myself. Show them all that I can make real runway fashion, and I belong in this class.

Show them that I'm on the right path.

I obsessively fixed every tiny detail I could see. I went to bed at one in the morning, and woke up at four to unpick and redo the shoddy seams. I waited outside the thrift store until it opened to hunt down exactly the right blood-red buttons. I even tore off the sleeve cuffs to remake them in lace—with a lot of swearing.

But it was what happened next that hurt the most.

Professor Meyer walked around my mannequin twice and scribbled in her notebook, looking distinctly disappointed. I remember the sinking feeling like a stone in my gut, dreading her feedback…

It was even worse than I expected.

"It's a D-worthy project, Ronan. It doesn't improve your portfolio."

Fuck

It still hurts. Every time I see this shirt, it brings back the scorned fury… and the humiliation of listening to my roommates snicker, riding high on their As. Do I really want to bring *that* vibe to my new home?

It's way too big for me to wear, anyway. I was hoping to summon a hunky man by using a hunky mannequin. I should just stuff it in the black garbage bag of clothes for the donation bin.

But even beyond the sentimental value of my family's repurposed clothes… I can't let it go. Like there's something else—a secret, buried treasure in its seams.

If there is, it's too deep for my teachers to find it.

"D-worthy," I grunt, holding it at arm's length and squinting.

Huh. Now that I've allowed those memories in—and through me—I can really look at it with fresh eyes. And…

something's wrong. Not the seams, buttons, or fit... much worse.

It's the concept.

Off-the-rack, my roommates sneered at me for weeks afterward. They're wrong, but *I'd* wear this in public these days. Maybe even in an office, on casual Friday. It wouldn't fly at my family's firm... but somewhere more laidback, I bet it would be a conversation piece that wouldn't get me fired.

I chose officewear, and made it into slightly unconventional officewear.

"Ohhhh, fuck." I sit back on my heels, reeling as it hits me like a ton of bricks: Professor Meyer was right.

It's a compromise. And what's the one rule of runway design? *Be uncompromising.*

I thought that wasn't a problem for me. After all, my greatest fear is waking up one day, opening a closet filled with identical dress shirts and shiny black shoes, and realizing that I've spent so long pretending to be someone else that it's become the truth.

Maybe I'm already on that slippery slope.

A chill runs down my spine despite the heat in my drafty old room.

"No," I breathe out defiantly, tossing the shirt into the suitcase. Decision made: I'm keeping it. I slam the suitcase shut and stand up, fists curled as I breathe hard. "I won't let that happen. Not ever."

That creative spark has always burned bright, in every bone of my body. I have to believe that it's good enough... that *I'm* good enough.

I'm a hell of a lot more than D-worthy.

CHAPTER
Thirteen

RONAN

I'm packed and waiting by the door.

I don't think I have long enough to sneak to the bathroom for another quick Alph-related fantasy, but I do have time to look around and say goodbye to one home, even if it never really felt like home.

It wasn't the house's fault. Without Alph here, it's not lovingly restored and improved like his place… but it was okay. It was always my roommates who were the problem.

I won't miss it here.

My new home is bright and exciting, full of potential—sexual and otherwise—and above all, peaceful. I can't believe I'm going to pay the same rent to live somewhere so much nicer, but Alph wasn't willing to hear otherwise.

As I stare down the hall into the kitchen, I hear the screen door on the porch open.

He's back!

I grab my suitcases by the handle, but then I catch a glimpse through the lace curtains on the front door and my heart plummets so fast that it leaves a crater in my stomach.

Fuck. It's not Alph. It's Derek.

He's the meanest of my three classmates, the one who spent the whole first year pretending not to remember my name. If we're alone in the house together, we always find a way of magically never being in the same place at the same time. It's better that way.

I jump back from the door just in time as he flings it open, then stops short to stare at me.

"The fuck, dude?"

I brace myself and take a deep breath. On the boat ride over, Alph gave me good advice about what to do if they were home: *The less said, the better.*

He laughs abruptly. "Class starts on Monday. Are you going on vacation?" He pulls a mocking sympathetic face. "Did the doctor tell you to take time off for stress?"

He's going to keep going until I say something, so I shrug and answer as blandly as possible. "No."

It's easier than I expected. For the first time, I can detach from the guy's words and see them for what they are: cheap jabs. Maybe he feels threatened by what I could do if I stop holding myself back. Well, he's in for a real surprise.

"Finally came to your senses and quit?" he jeers as he kicks his shoes off to wander down the hall.

"No." I check my watch—it's fifteen past, and Alph said he'd be back around now.

Derek snorts. He heads down the hallway, and then he stops dead. He's staring into my room. My now-empty room, stripped of everything but the furniture.

Shit. I close my eyes for a second, kicking myself. I should have closed it after me, but I didn't think anyone would come home yet.

Derek storms back to the door. "What the hell?" he shouts at me. "Are you moving out?"

"Yes."

That's it—I'm going to wait outside on the street. It's a nice day, and Derek doesn't have the guts to say this kind of shit in public where anyone could overhear.

I pull the inside door open, but Derek grabs the handle of one of my suitcases. I whirl toward him, narrowing my eyes so fast that he actually flinches back.

"Let go."

Derek sneers at me. "We'll have to get another roommate. You can't fuck us over like this!"

"I don't have to do this, but I left next month's rent in an envelope," I tell him perfectly calmly. "If you don't let go of my personal property right now, I'll go get it."

He stares at me, clearly dumbfounded that I'm standing up for myself.

So am I, but what is he going to do to me? Yell at me? Say mean things? Pretend he doesn't know my name? I don't give a shit what he says anymore. He has no power over me anymore, and he never really did.

Derek's greed takes over. He lets go and runs down the hallway to the kitchen. "You'd better not take anything that's ours!"

I roll my eyes and heft my other suitcase to the closed-in porch, and then I yank open the screen door.

I'm not taking anything that isn't mine. Unlike Derek and his posse, *I'm* not a vacant shell of a human being, and I won't let him drag me down with them.

There! It's Alph's car!

The little beater is practical, but it's a terrible mid-90s shade of brown. The prettiest thing about it is the bumper, which is covered in stickers about Sunrise Island. Some are faded, and others look almost new. *I <3 Sunrise Island, Get Away to Sunrise…* you get the idea.

My favourite is the sticker that says, *My Other Car is the Sunrise Island Ferry.* Alph has hand-written the ferry sailing times in Sharpie at the bottom of the sticker, which is the most Alph thing I can imagine.

Derek bursts into the screened-in porch and stares at me, envelope shoved firmly in his pocket. "We don't want to live with some rando all year!"

Knowing that Alph is just down the street makes me a little bolder, so I lift my first suitcase to the sidewalk and turn to him. "Maybe you should have thought about that *before* trying to make my life a misery."

Derek bares his teeth at me, while I just raise my eyebrows.

Considering how much he hates my guts, I figured he'd be glad to ditch the loser and find someone cooler to hang out with his squad. He must be real mad about losing his punching bag.

"You think your life was a misery before?" Derek laughs harshly. "I'll make sure it is now."

We both know his threats are empty. He and his cronies aren't just petty… they're lazy. See also: our household chore list, usually done by me alone.

"Get ready to come last in the showcase. Everyone's going to laugh at you, loser. You can't come up with an original idea to save your life—"

As the car pulls up, I lift the second suitcase over the threshold. "See you in class," I say, letting the screen door slam shut in his face as I wheel my suitcases toward the curb.

Alph doesn't even shut off the car. He just barrels out of

the driver's seat, rushing up to me like he's prepared to throw punches. "Are you okay?" he demands, stepping between me and the house and looking up at the porch.

I follow his gaze and laugh, because Derek is suddenly nowhere to be found. Dimes to donuts, he saw a guy much bigger and tougher than him and now he's hiding on the floor.

Good. He deserves a taste of his own medicine.

"I'm okay," I promise Alph, tapping his shoulder. "Come on. Help me with these."

He reluctantly turns to look at me, looking adorably disappointed to miss the chance to fight for my honour. "You're sure?"

"Positive."

Alph studies me, and something in my grin finally makes him relax. "Okay," he concedes, finally letting his breath out. He takes both suitcases and rolls them up to the car to lift them in.

I should help, but then I'd miss the chance to see his muscles doing... that thing, and suddenly I'm transfixed. Literally. It's not my fault. I just can't do anything besides stare at him and memorize what I'm seeing.

Alph must work out morning and night. Does he have a gym in his apartment downstairs? I wouldn't participate, but I'd totally pay money to watch him...

"With everything those assholes have done, they deserve to be punched," Alph interrupts my train of thought, slamming the trunk closed. He glowers at the house again. "Just say the word."

"Thank you, but there's really no need. I'm going to beat them fair and square."

Alph strides up to me out of the blue, and I squeak with surprise as his arms wrap around me.

I half-expect him to open the car door and lift me inside like a big old-fashioned suitcase. Instead, he squeezes me so tight he lifts me off the ground a little before setting me down again.

"Thattaboy," he growls. "Time to get to work."

Oh, my god.

I stare up at him, tongue-tied. Now that I know how easy it is for Alph to pick me up and heft me around, I'm going to need some alone time… and a lot of it.

All I can imagine is him shoving my head down on my cock, growling at me to get to work. Not that he'd need to order me around. I'd work my ass off for a glimpse of Alph letting go of his worries, giving in to his instinct, his need, his raw desire…

Alph opens the passenger door of the car and flourishes. "Your carriage is here, sir."

"I—uh—thanks," I squeak. I tumble into the seat and reach for the seatbelt, keeping one arm over my lap.

Alph closes the door and heads around to the driver's side, and I roll my head back, keeping my hands folded on my lap.

Think unsexy thoughts. Think unsexy thoughts. Think unsexy thoughts…

We're both quiet all the way to the seafront parkade. It's an open-walled concrete building with enough parking for everyone who lives, works, and plays at the harbour. Alph drives into a spot that overlooks Sunrise Island and shuts off the car.

I glance over, and then I stare.

This is the first time I've seen him look at anything else

the way he watches me when he doesn't think I'm looking… like a pretty bird he can't quite understand, or a flower he's studying to draw later. Or a tree he's proud to have known all his life.

Alph catches my gaze and smiles. "This is it."

"Yeah." I grin back at him, unbuckling and opening my door. "I've turned the page on that chapter of my life."

"Ready to head home and start a new one?" Alph asks, his voice echoing from the concrete floors and ceilings.

It takes him a minute to unfold himself and get out of a hatchback that doesn't look like it should fit him, so I glance over the harbour again.

I've seen Sunrise Island so many times from the windows at my campus, perched on a hillside overlooking the harbour. But I've never appreciated it as much as I do now, watching it shimmer through the warm haze like it's welcoming me home.

When Alph emerges and slams the door, I grin at him.

"Are you kidding? I was born ready."

CHAPTER

Fourteen

ALPH

SUMMER REALLY IS ALMOST OVER. RONAN'S FIRST DAY BACK AT college is tomorrow, and I'm happy for him. I really am. But I can't stop thinking about how much I'll miss having him around all the time.

It's bittersweet, but that was always the deal. Ronan is destined for great things. He's going to be busy sewing his heart out, running between classes, and who knows what else? I'm just being greedy, wanting to spend as much time as I can around him.

There's just one more thing left to do: I have to give him the tour.

Ronan has wandered around Sunrise on his own, but there's so much more to know about this place. He loved the idea when I suggested it over breakfast, so after work, I spent the afternoon making us a picnic, while Ronan sneakily wandered through the kitchen to nibble at whatever I make.

I think we're finally ready.

I'm not going to re-check the backpack again. This isn't

the wilderness. I can come back for anything in fifteen minutes, if it's that important.

"We're ready to go," I call out, but I don't get an answer.

I shoulder the backpack, sticking my head through the living room doorway.

I can't help my smile.

Ronan's already made himself at home in the living room. Half of it is taken up with his sewing machine, boxes of schoolwork, materials, and who knows what else. The other half is like an artist's studio, and currently covered in papers with sketchy lines and bursts of colour.

Despite what he said to me and Carter, he won't yet show me any of his work. He gets all embarrassed and mutters things about how it's not ready to see the world, so I want to respect him… but I can also see some of it from here.

And I don't know much about anything, but it looks good to me.

So does Ronan. He's lying on his front on the couch, humming softly to himself. He's bent his knees and crossed his ankles to wave his legs up and down in the air like a mermaid. But the best part is watching him furiously scribble in his notebook, nose scrunched with concentration.

It makes my heart melt to see him like this—happy and in his element.

Safe, at last.

"Oh!" Ronan looks up abruptly and launches himself up, nearly stumbling over the side of the couch. "Nothing here is final!"

I laugh and cover my eyes. "It's okay, I'm not looking. Just guide me to the stairs if you're ready to go."

Ronan giggles from nearby, in that soft sound that always makes me smile. "It's okay," he says, touching me on the shoulder. Everywhere his fingers touch prickles with pleasant heat. "You can look that way. Just don't… *look*, look."

"I won't look, look," I swear solemnly, hand on heart. "Just look. Maybe look, and then at a later moment, look. But not look, look."

Ronan snorts with laughter and shoves my shoulder. He can't budge me, but I pretend to stagger away from him. "Come on, goofball. Let's go."

"Hey. That was my idea," I protest.

Ronan grins. "We'll call it a collaboration." He skips down the stairs to the landing, and he's out the door before I even make it to the bottom. "So, where are we going first?"

I grin and tug the door closed. "Anywhere at all." But Ronan doesn't move. He's just standing there, looking pointedly between me and the door.

"Oh," I groan and fish around in my pocket for the keys. "I thought your serial killers strike at night. Okay, okay. Hold on."

I'll never get used to locking the doors. In a place where everyone knows everyone, most of us don't. It's easier to get help in an emergency that way, or just grab a cup of sugar when the store's closed.

But Ronan doesn't do things the Sunrise Island way yet, and that's okay. It'll come in time.

"They can strike at all hours," Ronan insists, his eyes sparkling as he falls into step beside me to head down the path. "I was listening to this episode today—"

"Oh, no, you don't," I interrupt him, wagging a finger. He told me way too much over supper last night. "If you want to scare yourself with all those podcasts, go ahead. I don't want any part in it."

I'm not going to admit that I spent the first few hours in

bed last night flinching at every familiar noise in my old house.

Ronan giggles at me and pulls the gate open. "It's okay for you. You can just punch an intruder in the face. *I* have to *flirt* my way out of the situation."

Ronan splays himself along the front gate and spreads his legs, tilting his head back. Watching him stand there in those little short-shorts, with his crop top and sandals, a sun-bronzed tinge to his face, the sunlight catching his blond hair…

Fuck. He's spellbinding.

I shake my head hard to pull myself out of it. "Did you put on sunscreen?" Ronan's chin flops back down against his chest and he groans, so I hold up my hands. "Sorry, sorry. Just making sure."

"I was busy fantasizing, you know," Ronan closes the gate and trots to catch up with me. "It's gone now. Ruined. I demand compensation."

"How about a tour?"

Ronan lights up like he's forgotten why we're going out for a walk. "Oh, yeah! When does the tour start? Or… where?"

I laugh and spread my arms to gesture around us. "Like I said… anywhere."

"Right here," Ronan declares in a low moan. "I'm ready, Alph. Hurry."

I'm not going to fall for that, either.

"Okay," I tell him, pointing out the house ahead of us. "So, the old mine shafts run in the woods behind this house…"

Ronan pouts to himself about me not taking the bait. It's very cute—and more than a little satisfying. I'm starting to learn the rules of his game. Sometimes I can even play it well enough to beat him, and that makes it more fun for us both.

God knows I'd love to let him have his way with me… but I can't let him get himself hurt, especially with his future to think about. For now, this has to stay exactly as it is: fun. Otherwise, our hearts might just get tangled up in all of this.

And then who knows what could happen?

CHAPTER

Fifteen

ALPH

"So, just to make sure..." Ronan giggles. "You're saying it *wasn't* you and your band of Sunrise Brothers who stole that scarecrow." He points at the raggedy old thing still planted in the soil at an increasingly unstable angle.

"Correct."

"And you don't know who dressed it in a bikini and put it in the top of the old lighthouse."

I grin at him. "I couldn't possibly tell you."

"Where it was seen by everyone passing by, and a whole tour group of historians from the provincial archives, until *someone* figured out how to open the window from the outside and get it back out again."

"Which was obviously how the culprits got it in there in the first place. And," I add, holding up a finger, "those are all original glass panes, so they were very careful. You might even say..." I pause for emphasis, "they took great pains." Then I grin at him. "Panes? Pains?"

"I am not acknowledging that," Ronan says. "Hey, are those apple trees? It's like a jungle in here."

"Yeah." I'm still proud of myself for that joke, whatever he says. "This is the old cider orchard. It got planted when the first people moved here. Sunrise cider was a big thing, like, fifty years ago? Sixty?" I shrug. "There even used to be a festival. By the time I was a kid... it just looked like this."

"That's so sad," Ronan murmurs, brushing his hand along a tree trunk. "Someone should look after it. Just for history's sake, you know?"

The wistful look on his face makes my heart squeeze gently. I like knowing that he feels the same way I do about this stuff. "As it happens, I heard that some young guy's bought it," I tell him. "He wants to restore the orchard and sell Sunrise cider again."

Ronan beams at me. "Really? Wait. Should we be walking here, then?"

"Oh, we're fine," I laugh. "Nobody's going to stop using the shortcut down to the beach. The real estate agents warn mainlanders about that stuff now. We had an incident a few years back. A mainlander moved here, and there was a trail through the corner of their land. They fenced it off one day without warning."

"Oooh," Ronan breathes out. "What happened?"

"Well, you can walk around, but it takes another five minutes. A lot of people missed their ferries. There was a real appetite for revenge. The next weekend was the pie auction, and..." I shake my head. "He got shunned. So badly, in fact, that he bought his own pie for twice the going rate, and then he took down the fence that night. By the next day, he'd turned it into a bench."

Ronan bursts out laughing as he clambers over the biggest stones at the edge of the beach. "Shunned at the pie auction? The *pie* auction? Is this real life?"

"I told you about the pie auction, didn't I?" I scramble after him, awkwardly swinging my legs over and sliding so I don't shake up the contents of our picnic.

"I might have missed it, among all the other events. Like the 'golf cart parade'," Ronan air-quotes, "and the 'bathtub race'—"

"They're real! Stay here long enough and you'll see."

We're finally on the smaller stones, where it will be easier to walk to the spot I've got in mind for our picnic... the perfect way to finish the perfect day.

I've never talked so much in the span of a few hours, but Ronan has been the best audience. He laughs at all the right moments. When he asks questions, it makes my heart *really* warm and fuzzy, because I think he's starting to care about this place the way I do.

And then maybe he *will* stay... until he graduates? Or longer?

I can only hope.

"Maybe I will," Ronan says at last, and then he chuckles. "If you still want me around. I know I'm getting a good deal—"

"Oh, man," I shake my head. "Trust me, I'm getting a better deal. Every time I thought about renting out the upstairs unit to someone I didn't know..." I puff a sigh through my lips. "I just couldn't bring myself to do it."

Ronan nods. "Downstairs doesn't have as many memories, does it? Why not switch around?"

"I thought about it, but I felt like I wasn't the right person to live there, either."

Ronan shakes his head. "You've looked after it so carefully. You care about it. Why not?" He's looking at me like he's not talking about just the house, but I can't figure out why.

"If it's a gallery… I'm the custodian," I tell him. "Not the artist." Then I stumble to a halt and stare at him. "Oh."

"Hi," Ronan waves at me with a mischievous little grin. "I'm an artist."

I nod slowly. "Yeah. You are."

That's what the place needed to feel alive again, like it did when I was growing up. Not another coat of paint, or another old radiator painstakingly swapped out… but someone who's got a big enough, sparkly enough personality to fill it up.

Like Ronan.

It's not just the living room piled high with fabrics, magazines, and vision boards. The guest bedroom walls are covered in an array of Blu-tacked sketches that he seems to rearrange every day. The fridge is filled with quick snacks he can grab on his way to class.

He just seems to belong there, like he always has.

I start walking again, and Ronan looks over at me. "For what it's worth… I think I'll be happy there."

"Yeah," I agree. "You will." And like that, we've arrived right at the one thing I've been trying to figure out how to bring up. "Speaking of which, if you don't need any more help settling in… I'll move back downstairs."

"Oh," Ronan says, over the crunch of our footsteps on the beach. And for once, I can't figure out how he feels about it.

The last thing I want to do is close the door at the bottom of the stairs, but it's time to let him live his fabulous, sparkly life.

No matter how much it seems like the house *wants* to be open… like it breathes better that way. It's just my mind playing tricks, because I remember the house before the basement became an apartment at all.

Nothing can stay the same forever.

"How about one more night?" Ronan tells me softly, hooking his arm around mine and batting his lashes up at me.

I stare down at him, my tongue suddenly clumsy against the roof of my mouth. It's hard when he suddenly touches me—whether he's pressing up against me, or softly running his hand over my skin.

Any way he touches me, my brain turns to mush.

"I'm not used to living alone," Ronan wheedles. "And I'm afraid of all the noises in the woods."

I swallow hard and rest my hand on his, trying to be casual about it. If walking arm-in-arm can ever be casual.

"Maybe you should stop listening to scary podcasts before bed."

"It wouldn't be a problem if I had a big, strong man to cuddle it better," Ronan tells me with great big puppy eyes.

Okay, now I can't argue with him. I'm too busy imagining how perfectly he'd fit into my lap. How much I'd love to pull him into my chest. Or even reach around to the front of his jeans and distract him thoroughly, until neither of us can hear any noises from outside at all...

"Alph?" Ronan whispers, coming to a halt.

I stare at him in a daze. "Huh?"

Even if we close the door between us... this thing between us isn't going to go away in a hurry. All it takes is one touch too many, and suddenly I can't call up a single anecdote, or funny joke, or another way to deflect his attention. Carter's right. I can't keep Ronan at arm's length forever.

It's impossible to stick to my ground when it's slipping under my feet like sand.

What do I *really* want?

That's an easy answer. Ever since I saw Ronan on Maple Island, the answer's been the same. I want to grab him, pull him into me, and never let him go. And here he is, asking me to do exactly that.

"One night?" Ronan says, all soft and nervous and sincere.

"Yes." My voice is hoarse to my own ears. "One night."

This might be the first time in my life I've been so happy to say yes to something that's so completely unknown—so unknowable, until we create it together.

Ronan's smiling at me, not saying anything.

I finally remind myself to let go of his arm… but he just runs his hand down my arm until he reaches my hand. His soft, delicate palm slides over my callouses until he finally slips his fingers in the spaces between mine.

Now that I've started wanting... I just can't help myself.

I curl my fingers around his, and I hold on tight.

CHAPTER
Sixteen

RONAN

MY BELLY IS FULL OF DELICIOUS FOOD, AND THE SUN IS sinking behind the trees.

It feels like we're a million miles from anywhere, gazing out over the flat blue sea and the rising tide. Alph calls this place Brothers' Cove. But it's a perfect place for lovers, too. There's plenty of room for both of us and the remnants of our picnic.

"Mm?" Alph offers me the wine bottle. It could feel tacky, drinking it without glasses, but instead it just fits the mood tonight.

"Mmhmm." I take it and prop myself up on my elbow against the smooth stones.

Now and then, I'll take his hand or he'll let his hand rest on my thigh. Neither of us have leaned in for a kiss yet… but all it takes is one look in each other's eyes to know that all our unspoken promises are still floating in the air between us.

Soon, I'll finally discover what they mean.

I'm so contented just to exist in the here and now with

Alph as the wine dwindles and the waves slowly rise to swallow the stony beach.

Sometimes one of us will say something, and we'll talk for a while—about our pasts and our futures, or about something that doesn't matter much at all. But it's just as nice to be quiet. I don't feel the need to chatter and show off and make dirty jokes.

I'm not trying to catch Alph's eye and earn his attention. I've already done that—I've got him. Hook, line, and sinker.

"Hm?" I ask Alph, glancing over to offer him another turn with the wine bottle.

But he's still propped up on his elbow, studying me intensely. He looks like he's trying to plot a course on a map, desperately searching for a star or a landmark to figure out how to make sense of me.

And I get it.

Until he brought me to this place, I think there was something about him that I didn't understand.

I've tumbled chaotically into Alph's life, and now that I can finally relax... I'm starting to appreciate its pace. The tide comes and goes, one season slowly turns into another, and all things grow at the speed they're supposed to.

Alph shakes his head to turn down the wine, and I shrug and take another sip. "How does this whole thing work? With your first collection and the runway showcase?" he asks instead.

It makes me feel so warm and fuzzy that he wants to know, and that's an easy question. So I scoot back to sit cross-legged, leaning back against a boulder as Alph stays on his back to listen to me.

"Ideally, the work we did last year in the portfolio class is our foundation. But I'm scrapping the whole thing and starting from scratch."

Alph's eyes widen. "Seriously?" He isn't saying it like it's a bad idea—he's just shocked.

"Yeah." I smile. "The more I look at it, the more I realize what I was doing wrong."

"What's that?"

I sigh. "Compromising. I always run after what I want. But I was so afraid of ending up with nothing at all…" I trail off.

That I try to give other people what I think they want. I push myself right to the limit of what I can tolerate.

A roommate arrangement that gives me sewing space, even if it means they get a punching bag. A shirt that feels daring to me, but it's still close enough to my family's world that they'll understand what it means. A hot rendezvous where I feel desired, but they don't have to keep me around.

I look down at Alph, who just smiles gently at me, and suddenly the rising itch of discomfort settles down again.

"So." I clear my throat. "I'd rather fail by taking a risk and doing something I'm proud of. Even if my roommates kick my ass and gloat about it later."

Alph pushes himself up on an elbow, frowning with genuine confusion. "Why do you think they'll do better?"

"They always do. Especially last year, when the teachers started marking us tougher. I try to come up with original ideas, and they do something similar that looks way better."

Alph grunts. "That doesn't make sense. You've got ten times the imagination of anyone I know."

"Yeah. But I don't have the same technical skills."

It stings my pride to admit, but I've always been more of a designer than a maker. I'm always the one who manages to do a seam inside-out, or forget that I'll need a zipper in the back of a dress.

"I didn't know how to drive a ferry until, oh… six months ago." Alph smiles up at me. "You can learn fast."

"Yeah. My roommates got better really quickly once they got a studio and started working on their brand," I roll my eyes. "But that's not what worries me… it's the concept. What if they keep coming up with my ideas, but making them better?"

Wait.

I stop and stare across the water. My brain is whirring at a thousand miles an hour.

That's what always happens, over and over. The menswear project. The evening gala dress. The historical costume. Isn't that a little bit… weird?

"What?" Alph says. He scoots back over the stones to sit next to me, pressing both of his hands around mine. "Ronan?"

His touch helps ground me, keeps me just calm enough to think straight. I gulp as he squeezes me and rubs circles against the back of my hand like he's trying to warm me up.

"Let me think," I whisper, shaking my head dizzily. "Their final projects last year. Breanna… she used old pieces of curtain and silk ties. Patchwork, sort of like me." That's an awfully shaky premise so far.

"Uh huh."

"Shane sewed a cape into, like, a bubble that floated around the model…" My heart leaps into my throat, and my hands won't stop shaking. "Over a jumpsuit. Sewed up to look like officewear. Dress shirt, trousers, tie… all in black and white panels. Like me."

Fuck. How come I didn't see before?

"What about the third one?" Alph asks, prying the wine bottle away from me. He rests his palm on my knee. "Derek?"

"A see-through wedding gown. With an opaque veil and train… all in blood-red lace…"

I take a deep breath as the last scrap of my uncertainty vanishes. I feel like I just got hit in the stomach with a cannonball, but at last I know what's happening.

"Just like me," I finish.

Alph's nostrils flare. He sits upright and shoves the bottle firmly into the stones so it stands upright, then turns to face me fully. "They're copying you?"

"They must be." I shake my head. "But why? They're always saying how much better they are…"

Alph shakes his head, squeezing my knee until I look at him. "Don't worry about that yet. Do you know *how*?"

"My portfolio," I whisper. "I guess it would be easy. My process is… messy."

Alph's lips twitch. "It spreads all over the room?"

"Sometimes I lose drawings, and I swear I can't find them, but they come back. They're always barging in when I sew. Trying to annoy me…" I trail off.

"Or trying to see what you're doing." Alph grimly nods, and I nod back. I feel sick. "So why the hell haven't they gotten caught?"

I sigh. "It's subtle. It's not one-for-one copying. Sometimes people have similar ideas—that's not unusual. It was just consistently the three of them, all year long, doing similar things but sewing them better."

"*Are* they sewing them?" Alph raises his eyebrow. "If they don't even want to come up with their own ideas…" he trails off meaningfully.

"There's assignments in class—" I cut myself off, and then

I clear my throat. "And they fuck around like arrogant dickheads. Acting like they're too good to be there. They go away and fix their mistakes later."

Alph nods with grim triumph. "Or they're getting someone else to redo it."

They always said they could do anything twice, better than I could do it once. The words suddenly ring hollow in my mind. I feel so much better about myself.

"Yes," I laugh, unable to explain the intoxicating relief. "Yeah. You're right!"

Alph is furious enough for both of us. "Fuckers," he growls. "I knew I should have punched them. Thank god they can't spy on you anymore!"

I shudder. My skin crawls, I feel so violated. "They must have been in my room all the time! Urgh."

"You gotta turn them in." Alph's eyes are glinting with fury. "It's wrong. Your teachers will want to know."

He's not going to like my answer.

I bite my lip and look out over the water, then back at Alph. Maybe," I tell him. I don't want my first day of class to be overshadowed by something that's so hard to prove now. "I don't have real evidence."

Alph fidgets with the stones between us, a pained look on his face. "But it's wrong."

"I know." I fold up my legs, turning to sit cross-legged facing Alph. Then I lean over him and grab the wine bottle and gulp down another mouthful. "You wanna know the good news?" I grin smugly. "They've screwed themselves. They'll never see my portfolio again. Only what I do in class… and the showcase, when I kick their asses."

The storm cloud hanging over Alph's head steadily

brightens, until he finally nods. "Here's to kicking their asses," he says and gently fistbumps the wine bottle.

I crack up. "Is that a toast?"

"Sure is. Quick, you go first," Alph urges me. As I take a swig, he raises his fist. "To kicking their asses." Once I've swallowed, he grabs the bottle and takes a gulp, looking up at me pointedly. "Mmph-fff—" he waves his hand in a *hurry up!* gesture.

I can't stop giggling at how ridiculous this is. "To kicking their asses!" I wheeze.

Alph swallows and groans with relief. "Sorry I didn't bring glasses."

"Did you actually forget something? *You?*" I tease him, scooting closer and grabbing his shoulders to hoist myself up on his lap.

Alph wraps one big, strong arm around my back, keeping me in place as I tingle with anticipation. "No," he answers. "It was deliberate. I was worried they'd break, and the glass would hurt someone on the beach."

That makes my heart flutter strangely. I beam down at him and shake my head. "That's a very Alph thing to say."

"Hey," he snorts. "I'm nothing if not predictable. At least you know what you're getting." His voice is light, but his words sound like they're carefully, deliberately chosen.

Even more so than usual.

Yeah. I do know what I'm getting.

Alph just makes sense. I can trust what he says because I can trust what he does—and I trust that he's made sure it's the right thing to do.

Even if I take him by surprise sometimes.

"What's wrong with this, anyway?" I murmur, catching

Alph's gaze before I lean in over the mouth of the bottle he's holding midair.

His eyes snap wide open. His Adam's apple bobs, and the bottle twitches midair. He takes a deep breath, steadying it again as his arm tightens around my back. And I still don't look away—not until the last possible moment.

Then, I wrap my lips around the mouth of the bottle, keeping my teeth well out of the way as I suck the neck into my mouth, an inch at a time. When I'm almost kissing the spot where the bottle widens, I slowly straighten up again and suck my cheeks in.

Pop!

With a wet noise, my mouth slides free.

I shoot Alph a sultry gaze and flick my tongue across my lower lip, provoking him… waiting to see what he'll do.

The tension rolls between us like the unending surf before us. Blue, stretching out for miles and miles, so vast that it could swallow us whole and never let go.

Slowly, Alph raises the wine bottle.

He wraps his lips around the glistening glass and pauses… like he's tasting me. He sucks it into his mouth— just the tip, but certainly more than he needs to—and he tips his head back to swallow a gulp of wine.

That's the hottest thing I've ever seen.

I stare at Alph as he lowers the bottle again and silently catches my gaze again.

My heart is thudding too fast. My pants feel tight, and it could be my imagination… but I think there's something rising in his expression.

"Nothing," Alph whispers, and for a moment I can't even remember the question. "Nothing's wrong with this, Ronan."

I can hardly breathe, just trembling with anticipation. I'm fighting with all I have against my urge to grab Alph and pull him into me, to make him acknowledge what I want from him… because there's something else we both need even more.

Alph has to take what he wants.

In the blink of an eye, Alph slams the wine bottle into the stones and grabs the back of my head. His fingers tangle into my hair, exactly as gentle and as rough as I dreamed they would be, and he leans back and yanks me into his chest. I fall into him… but he's right here to catch me.

Our lips meet, and it's nothing like before.

Alph kisses me hard and fast. His hot mouth glides across mine, claiming it as his territory. My lips part, and he seizes the lower lip between his own, dragging his teeth across it as sparks flash behind my eyes.

My body aches with a need for him—so great that it spills out of me, too beautiful to want to control. I whimper and press helplessly against him, but I can't quite find a way to grind against his hip.

I'm too busy melting as he explores my mouth. He pushes his tongue between my lips, and then he gives a soft growl of delight as our tongues slide against each other in a hot, awkward clash of mouths. He pulls back, nips my upper lip, and then goes back to flicking his tongue against my lower lip.

Noises spill out of me unbidden. I'm trembling, writhing against him. My nails dig into his shoulders as I beg for more…

And Alph doesn't stop.

He just keeps kissing me like I've never been kissed—

exactly like I need to be kissed to forget about tomorrow, and everything that comes after.

The only thing that matters is tonight.

CHAPTER
Seventeen

ALPH

Eventually, Ronan and I need to breathe, which doesn't seem fair.

We're magnets that have finally found the right way to each other. It's impossible to pull ourselves apart.

As we gasp for breath, my lips want so badly to linger on his—if only so I can taste the air going into his lungs. Our foreheads are still touching, and the tips of our noses. Nor can I let go of the back of his head. It fits so perfectly against my palm, like it was always meant to be there.

I'm stunned. I can barely believe what I did… but it feels so right.

Is *this* what it's like to go after what you want?

It's intoxicating. It's terrifying. It's… perfect.

Ronan moans again—soft, needy—and I'm lost.

Instinct pulls me into him. We're kissing again, my hand sliding down to the small of his back, and then up again to explore the flat plane of his back. Then, I shove myself away from the boulders to lie flat on my back.

I don't have to work hard to pull Ronan on top of me. He's eager, quick to straddle my hips.

As he pushes down against my thighs, I groan.

He's as hard as me. I can feel the length of him desperately straining against his pants, grinding into my thigh.

It makes my head spin. I've never felt this before, and I want so badly to feel it a thousand times again. Over and over, I want to make him hard and then pull me into him so I can revel in what I've done.

He grabs my face, pressing his mouth to mine in a burst of quick, fiery, insistent kisses that last no more than a breath. I retaliate by turning my head, kissing along his stubble-covered jaw to his ear, tasting him... exploring every spot that makes him tremble.

Our limbs tangle together as stones dig into my back, and I don't care.

I want this.

"Fuck," Ronan gasps, one hand curling around my wrist as he trembles above me. "Y-You're good."

It takes a minute to remember how to make my mouth do anything other than savour the taste of him, and drink in all the bliss that shines out from every cell of his body.

"Thanks," I grunt, nipping behind his ear. He squirms and makes another soft, tiny sound that makes me want to flip us over and press between his legs. I settle for raking my nails down his back. "I'm new... but enthusiastic."

Ronan's moan is low and guttural.

Jesus. My cock was already aching hard, but now it's throbbing relentlessly. I want to hear him make that noise over and over.

"I hope that extends beyond kissing," Ronan pants for breath.

I laugh, a quick puff of breath.

He really has no idea what fantasies he's pulling out of the furthest reaches of my body, and planting dead centre in my mind.

"It does," I promise him, running my nails slowly up his back. "It really, really does."

Ronan whimpers, one hand rising to his chest. I bask in the sight of the fading orange light catching his hair, the shadows against his body…

But I want to see more of him.

A *lot* more.

"Should we go home?" I murmur, even though it's not a question, or even really a suggestion.

Ronan's eyes open as he stares hazily down at me. He smiles playfully and whispers, "I thought you'd never ask."

It makes me remember that first night: all his flirtation, and my yearning, and the collision of duty and desire.

"Come on." Ronan pulls away from me to shove things into the backpack without much care at all. He doesn't even put lids onto containers… and, to my own surprise, I don't stop him. I join in.

In seconds, we're packed and on our feet. We stumble across the stones and through the trees, squinting in the growing gloom. When we reach the road, I set a quick pace, and Ronan holds on tight around my arm.

My mind is racing.

This is happening. In fact, I don't know if I can stop it from happening… and I probably should feel worse about that than I do.

It's a struggle not to freak myself out about it.

"Penny for your thoughts?" Ronan asks as we turn the final corner. He wriggles his fingers into my palm and traces circles on my skin, glancing up at me between steps.

I swallow hard and squeeze his hand in mine, trying to think how to say it.

"I don't know what you want from me," I admit at last. "But I know the one thing I can't do."

"Can't?" Ronan prods. "Or shouldn't? Or won't?"

I see why he's asking, but I don't know how to explain it. I pause, and then I try my best. "They're the same thing to me. Or as good as."

Ronan hums thoughtfully. "Okay. What can't you do?"

"Distract you," I tell him. "Get in the way." Before he can protest, I hold up my hand, asking for a chance to explain. "You have the opportunity of a lifetime—your whole future ahead of you. It all rests on the next couple of months. I'd never forgive myself for getting in the way of that." I squeeze his hand. "Ever."

Ronan bites his lip. "But... you wouldn't be in the way."

Oh, Ronan.

If there's one thing that defines Ronan at his best... I think that's it. Hope. It's one of the reasons I like him so much. But I can't let it cloud my judgment.

"I won't be," I promise.

Ronan glances at me as I let go of him to hold the gate open for us both. Then he does a double-take, like he's realizing what I actually mean, and slowly walks through it.

I follow after him, and then I take his hand again to lead him up the porch stairs, my heart aching.

It's not going to be easy.

But I don't do the easy thing. I do the thing that's right—and I can't even make myself do anything else. And what's right is making sure that Ronan has the time, the space, and the *unbroken* heart he needs to create the best work he's ever made.

I just don't know what that means for us… right now.

As we step inside, I set down the picnic bag. We kick our shoes off at the same moment, and then Ronan takes me by the hand and leads me upstairs. When we get to the top of the stairs, he stops.

Ronan turns to face me, and he takes my other hand, gazing up. "So… what *do* you want?"

I stare at him, not quite sure how the answer isn't already obvious. My whole body aches with it.

You.

Ronan chuckles and shakes his head. "Let me rephrase that. What would make you freak out less than you are right now?"

"Oh."

Thank god he didn't ask what I'm worrying about, or we'd be here all night. The list is so long that there's an abridged edition. It's got an index at the back. In hardback, it could knock a man unconscious in a single swing.

But if I had to pick the top worries, that's actually easy.

"I want to know what you're expecting."

Ronan smiles again. He tilts his face up at me. "Nothing," he says, and I can see the sincerity all over his face. "I *want*, yes. I hope. I fantasize, while jerking off in the shower…"

Oh… my… *god.*

I've spent the week hopelessly distracted by Ronan. Now that I know he's been jerking off to the thought of me, too… the sound of the shower is going to do *so* many things to me. Already, I'm hard again. Painfully so.

All I can see is Ronan naked under the water, one hand wrapped around himself as he tilts his head back and moans…

Ronan stretches up on his tiptoes and presses a kiss on

the dip between my collarbones. Then he settles onto his feet again. "But I don't *expect* anything. Tonight or ever. Just you, as you are... doing what *you* want to do, for a change."

I'm hanging onto his every word, nodding along.

Ronan pauses and squints at me. "For tonight, can you let yourself do that? Stop worrying about me?"

I lick my lips. "I will. As much as I can."

"Good." Ronan squeezes my hands. "Take what you want from me. Trust me, I want it too—every bit as bad as you do."

"Good," I echo him. "And there's one more thing. What happens after tonight?"

Ronan nods, his smile disappearing as he watches me earnestly. "Tonight is just tonight. We'll worry about everything else later."

Worry knots my chest. I'm trying to let his words sink in and reassure me, but it's hard.

Ronan can see it on my face. He winks up at me like he's trying to make me relax. "You can go back to batting me away when I make everything you say into a horny joke. I won't be offended."

I think he actually means it, too.

I let out a breath, and Ronan chuckles like he can see the relief all over me. His expression softens, and he tilts his face up toward me again, stepping close.

"Good?" he whispers.

My answer is a kiss—a long, deep kiss that feels like it will never end.

I kiss Ronan until his knees buckle. I kiss him until he's a whimpering puddle against me. I keep on kissing him, until my body is lost in the ache of my need to be on top of him and inside him, giving him all of me.

At last, when we're both swimming in the overwhelming

flood of desire, I walk him right backward down the hall to the bedroom.

Ronan moans when I kick the door closed, and then I push forward against him again, walking him to the edge of the bed.

I shove him onto it, and as he scoots backward, I fall on top of him.

Ronan grunts, grabs the top button of my shirt, and pulls it open. It's like something snaps between us—the last of our self-restraint.

Now, we only have the excitement, the hunger, the need…

The wanting. All of it. And I can't contain it anymore.

Ronan unbuttons my shirt as fast as he can. I wrestle his T-shirt off, hauling his arms up and clear. He shoves my jeans down while I fumble with the button on his, and he kicks his underwear off as soon as I get it down to his ankles.

As we tear each other's clothes off, I press down against him again. I feel like I'm on fire, everywhere our bare skin meets. The angles of his body against mine, the sharp force of his desire and the answering surge of mine… it's like nothing I've ever fucking come close to before.

My underwear is the last thing to come off. It's a relief to toss it aside, and I turn back to Ronan to grin down at him.

He's staring down with wide eyes, and my chest swells at the look on his face. Just having him watch me feels good. A strange, breathless pleasure pulsates through me until my dick twitches like it's standing to attention.

"Whoa," he breathes out, and I can't blame him.

I'm not small… and right now, I'm rock-hard. I just hope it's not too much.

I open my mouth to ask him if he's okay, but Ronan shoots me a little glance—a teasing warning.

Oh. Right.

What I want is what he wants.

I let go of the instinct to check on him. He *did* say how much he likes to be stretched, after all…

I'm still feeling pleased and proud—and maybe even a little bit cocky. So I lean into that, instead.

"You like seeing that?" I tell him, raising my chin to look him slowly up and down and drink in the sight. "Is this the dick you were daydreaming about?"

Ronan's jaw drops. He blushes furiously and squirms under me. He's hard, too, standing proud against his stomach. "Y-Yes," he gasps.

His voice rings through me, and suddenly I feel calm.

I have the power to give him everything he needs. If not the knowledge, certainly the enthusiasm and pure, raw desire to make up for it.

Ronan can't stop himself from looking down at my cock again, and the tip of his tongue peeks out over his lower lip.

I know how to take a cue.

"You're a good kisser, Ronan." I smirk at him. "I think it's time you showed me what pretty mouths like yours were made for."

Ronan's eyes are like dinner plates. His breathing turns into a harsh, open-mouthed pant as he parts his lips, openly staring at my manhood now. "Yes," he pants. "Please."

I'm already crawling up to straddle his chest, and he whimpers happily.

As if I'm giving in that easily. I may be eager, but I know how much he loves to work for it. It would be a shame not to reward him even more.

"What was that?" I tease him, sitting back on my heels instead.

Ronan's eyes fly open again. He's blushing right to the tips of his ears, staring up at me. "Please…?"

I grab his head and tangle both hands in my hair, pulling gently at the strands.

Ronan whimpers and bucks off the bed, scrabbling at the comforter. "Oh, fuck! Yes, please, please, *please!* Tell me to get to work," he pants. "I'll do it. Anytime you want."

That's very good to know.

I growl softly at him, running my fingertips behind his ears and along his jaw, tracing all the sensitive spots I found earlier. "Better."

"Please, Alph!" Ronan whimpers. "Please let me suck you off!"

I can see one hand wandering towards himself. I grin and pull it over his head, and then I grab the other wrist for good measure.

"Mmph!" Ronan grunts, squirming helplessly against me. At last, he collapses again and stares up at me. "Please…?"

I can't stand it anymore.

This is already the hottest thing I've ever done in my life.

I didn't know sex could be like *this*. Full of my wanting, *and* his wanting, and the way those things collide with one another and explode into something ten times hotter, ten times fiercer than we ever could have imagined.

Seeing his true desperation makes my heart softer… and my dick that much harder. As much as I want to tease him all night, Ronan looks too fucking gorgeous. He's giving me everything I ask for and then some.

Now it's time to give him what he wants.

I stroke his cheeks, cup his hair, run my hands along the

sides of his neck. I lean down, making sure he can hear me… and then I growl the words he's waiting to hear.

"Get to work."

Ronan gasps with relief as I shift my weight over him, bracing one forearm over his head. I lean against him, pushing my cock against the wet warmth of his lips…

And I'm inside.

Oh, fuck.

His mouth is so hot. So perfect. I couldn't have imagined any better. His tongue dances around the shaft, doing things that make my eyes roll back in my head. He sucks his cheeks in, and showers of sparks course through my body.

I push myself further and further into Ronan's mouth, entranced by the sight of his kiss-swollen lips stretching around my pink-flushed, veiny shaft. I stop just before his throat, but Ronan's hands are moving again—too fast for me to stop.

Ronan grabs my ass and pulls me into him, hard.

"Fuck!" I grunt. The head of my cock slides into the tightness of his throat. I throw my head back, gasping for breath as my body surges with heat.

I pull back a little, and Ronan keeps his hands on my hips. I think he's enjoying feeling my muscles flex under his palms as I fuck down into his mouth, slow and steady at first, and then faster.

In between the wet sound of me sliding into his mouth, Ronan's making the hottest little sounds.

"Nnh! Mmph! Nngh!" he whimpers, sucking his cheeks tightly around me. He keeps trying to steal peeks at me whenever he can.

And he's fucking *gorgeous*.

I'm not just saying that because I'm shamelessly using his

mouth, pushing myself deeper and deeper until his lips stretch around the base of my shaft.

It's because I've never seen Ronan like this before… like he's in his element. He's fiery and unstoppable, yes… but also pliable. I'm not too much for him—he wants to feel it all, the full force of my desire.

I can do that.

I'm overwhelmed with all these new sensations. My muscles are drawing tight, and I'm already a million miles past the peak of what I've ever known before, so I have no idea where the edge is going to be.

I just know I'm heading there, and fast.

"Nnh," I grunt, pulling out of Ronan's mouth. I slide down and straddle him without wasting a moment, grabbing both of our cocks in one hand.

I'm standing against the firmest part of my palm, but I have the weight of him against my fingertips, where I can feel him the best.

He's velvety and firm, but the length is a little more short and stout. The head of his cock is a gentle, beautiful point that runs easily over my fingertips, and the base is so thick I can hardly fit my hand around us both.

But the best part is how his cock feels sliding against mine.

It's fucking *incredible*.

"Yes," Ronan gasps as I start to jerk us off together. He scrabbles against my back, tipping his chin back to bare the curve of his throat. I can't tear my gaze off him as he whimpers and cries out at the top of his lungs.

I want to grind against Ronan until I've rubbed off on him for good— covered him with me in a way he'll never forget.

Then, Ronan's whole body heaves off the bed, forming the most perfect arc. "Yes…!"

My hips snap forward as I push into him and grind, squeezing both of us together as tight as I can. "Ronan…!"

"Yes yes *yes* oh fuck oh my god Alph yessss!" Ronan's voice breaks and he gasps silently.

Both of our cocks pulsate and throb in my hand.

It hits me, too. I can't stop it.

"Fuck!" I throw my head back as all my thoughts disappear in a tidal wave of *yes* and *fuck fuck fuck* and *Ronan!* We're burning up together, covering each other—and Ronan, from his collarbone to his belly button—in our sticky passion.

But it's Ronan's face I can't stop watching.

He looks like he can barely believe how good this feels. He looks blissful, helpless in my hands… and *perfect.*

When my cock finally starts to soften, I groan and slowly let go of us both. He whimpers one last time, a soft noise that I can't resist.

I collapse on top of him, already too coated in sweat and gleaming with ecstasy to care about the mess. All I care about is holding his body against mine while we're naked and soft and still spellbound by the moment.

"Mmm," Ronan whimpers, so softly that I don't know if he even knows he made the sound. He cuddles into me, presses his nose into my neck, and I wrap my arm around him to pull him closer.

He's melting my fucking heart.

I run my hand gently up and down Ronan's back, exploring the planes and angles.

How come every single one is this fucking perfect, anyway? How is that possible?

Ronan's hand slow rises to my chest, then over the

muscles there, until he curls it around my bicep. His eyes are still closed, and his lips are softly curved up in the most contented little smile.

It's the most beautiful thing I've ever seen.

At last—at long last—he looks like he might be falling asleep, so I nudge him. I can barely bring myself to disturb him, but I have to.

"Mm?"

"Shower," I murmur.

Ronan gives me a sleepy, adorable chuckle. "How responsible," he murmurs.

I laugh breathlessly, running my hand through his hair to pet it back into place. "Hey, I can't turn it off forever. Now, come on. Before you go to sleep."

Ronan groans in protest, but I know what to do. I slide to the edge of the bed and bend over to pick him up. He's lighter than I thought, and easy to cradle in my arms.

"Don't worry," I murmur, walking carefully toward the bedroom door. "I'll make sure you get there."

He just hums against my chest and nuzzles me.

Can he hear what that does to my pulse? Feel what it does to my heart?

There's no way I can even begin to worry about what happens next, or after that, or forever. Ronan was right. When tomorrow comes, we'll figure it out.

For tonight? I have everything I want.

CHAPTER
Eighteen

RONAN

I can't stop thinking about that night we shared… and imagining what's still to come. I think about it constantly—and so does my hand, several times a day, quite vigorously.

Who could blame me when it was so goddamn perfect?

I've never come so hard and fast that I saw stars. I've never had to be carried to the shower afterward. I've certainly never been set down gently on my feet, scrubbed all over, towelled dry, and carried right back to bed.

Just this once? Yeah, right.

It's only a matter of time. The pull between us is too strong. He's only living one floor below me. When I left for school, the door at the bottom of the stairs was open. Another moment will come where neither of us can stop it… and I have so many daydreams about what will happen next.

"Ronan! Oh my god, you look great! How are you?"

"Gabs!" I beam as the next classmate comes in the room, scrambling to my feet for a hug. "You made it back! I *am* great. Oh my god, look, it's Ophelia…!"

Every time someone comes through the door, the rest of

us cheer as we rush over to greet each other. I've known my classmates for three years now, and it's exciting to see who's made it back for this final, toughest year.

The first class of the year always feels like a party... at least, until Professor Meyer arrives. Right on cue, the door opens again.

"Good morning, class," Professor Meyer says as she strides in. We greet her much more calmly, hastily settling down at our desks.

My ex-roommates aren't here yet. I can dream, right?

As always, our professor is dressed to the nines—today, in fuchsia pumps, a bright yellow asymmetric jacket with an angled hem, and a single, fuchsia, enamel hoop in one ear. I flip my notebook open to scribble that down.

It's always worth studying Marsha Meyer's outfits. She's spent over forty years in the industry, and she's been teaching for... I don't know how long. Basically, she knows everyone and everything there is to know.

Professor Meyer heads up to the lectern and sets her briefcase on the floor, which is the signal that the lesson has begun. "Well..."

The door opens again.

Breanna, Derek, and Shane float inside without even looking at our teacher, much less anyone else. The rest of us have all sat in a row on one side of the semi-circle... but they all sit together and leave a gap of several desks.

Typical. I roll my eyes. I bet they realized last year that nobody gets excited to see an asshole. At least, not in this context.

Showing up late to Professor Meyer's class, though? That's a bold move.

Professor Meyer raises her eyebrows and stares in their

direction. We all hold our breaths, and the three of them sit down in a hurry.

"So," Professor Meyer says at last, folding her hands on her lectern and returning her gaze to the rest of us. "This is it. Twenty of you left this room last year. Fifteen came back."

I swallow hard and glance around furtively, like the rest of us are doing—checking who's missing.

"I'm not surprised at who left," Professor Meyer tells us, which grabs our attention again. "By the end of Portfolio Development 1, I can always tell. So… welcome, students, to Portfolio Development 2."

The name alone is infamous.

Her gaze is flicking between each of us, one at a time. "It will be a tough year," she tells us. "We have higher standards for our students than ever before."

She pauses and looks right at me… but I was expecting it. I don't flinch away. In fact, I deliberately smile and sit up a little straighter.

Her eyebrow raises… and then her gaze moves on, and I can relax.

"You've learned how to adapt, collaborate, and imitate in order to sustain a brand identity. You'll need those skills in your future. But this semester, you're going to learn something much more important. Which is…?"

Nobody says a word.

She sighs. "Ronan?"

I glance down at my notebook, but the answer is already on my lips. I remember her comments on my portfolio last year… word-for-word.

Often lacks the courage and vision of an original identity.

"Our own identity."

I can feel my former roommates smirking. They're

casting looks at me behind her back, and for a moment, my irritation *almost* rises. They love to keep track of all the times I get called out in class.

Usually, I blush and look down. Now, it rolls right off me. Their opinions don't matter. Besides which… I know their dirty little secret.

And I'm going to work at this twice as hard as they're willing to fake it.

Our teacher folds her arms and stares at me thoughtfully. "Good, Ronan."

I blink up at her. She… actually sounds like she means it. Did I pass some test I didn't know about?

"This is the year you discover your identity as a designer. It will change, of course. You'll refine it. Maybe you'll pivot altogether a few times in your career. But this is your starting point. So… I have an announcement that some of you will be happy about, and some of you… will not."

She unfolds her arms, coming out from behind the lectern to pace back and forth in front of us. "No more group projects."

Stifled gasps and murmurs greet her words, and then we hastily quiet down again.

"That's right." She smiles. "No more groups, or pairing up, or making anyone else carry you along." She pauses at the far end of the row, drumming her fingernails on Breanna's desk. She turns to study us all. "Nowhere to hide. Nobody to copy."

I can hardly breathe.

She isn't looking at my roommates. I'm trying not to look at them, either, but I'd bet my bottom dollar they're shitting bricks.

But she's striding back already, looking from face to face.

"Can't take the heat? Get out of the kitchen. For the rest of you, this is where *your* identity will be forged."

There's a hushed silence in the room. Some of us are smiling a little, and others look worried. My roommates are opening up their laptop—and their messaging programs, so they can talk to each other and pretend not to care about what's going on in class.

I'm the only one who's glowing with excitement, like it's day one of first year all over again.

She looks at me.

"Who are you going to be? What mark are you going to leave? What is it that you—and only you—can give the rest of us?"

That's it. I'm sure of it now. Now that I've seen my work with fresh eyes—and I'm not same the person who made those things anymore—I know why Professor Meyer said what she did at the end of last year.

She sees what I'm capable of, and what I've been holding back.

"Whatever that thing is that you have to offer, there's only one sin in this class: hoarding it for yourself. Because, by the end of the semester, you're going to have to be ready to share it with the world. Got it?"

We murmur in agreement.

"First assignment." She scoops up her briefcase and opens the snaps, pulling out an armful of folders. Her heels click briskly as she walks along the row, tossing a heavy folder onto each of our desks. "By the end of the semester, this is what you'll present me. These are portfolios, each show-casing a mini-collection from a well-known designer early in their careers."

I swallow hard and grab my folder, pulling it close to me.

"Study it tonight," she tells us. "Be ready to answer questions tomorrow."

Chairs squeak on the floor as we grab our backpacks and bags to shove the folders into. Professor Meyer strides back to the lectern and waits for us all to straighten up to begin the lesson in earnest.

All I can hear is Alph's voice in my head. *"You're going to be top of the class. I just know it."*

And suddenly, I have an idea.

I've been stressing out about not knowing what I needed to do, or how I can get better. But now that I have some of the answers… I know who has the rest of them.

This might be crazy. But it might just work.

CHAPTER
Nineteen

ALPH

ONE WEEK INTO THE SCHOOL YEAR, THE UPSTAIRS LIVING ROOM looks more like a workshop than a home.

I've been trying to keep my nose out of Ronan's business, but neither of us seems to want to close that dividing door between us. It's just more convenient to pop our heads upstairs or down to talk about our schedules or dinner plans.

Or if I hear an alarming amount of thudding and cursing.

"Ronan?" I take the last few stairs with caution. I can't even peek between the banisters—there are cardboard boxes in the way now.

Ronan's response is a strangled groan. I peek around the corner and catch my breath at the sight of him lying face-first on the floor.

Shit, is he—

"I'm too pretty for manual labour." Ronan rolls his head slowly until his cheek is squished on the floor, looking up at me. He's all sweaty and out of breath. "I borrowed a wheel-barrow. I'm never doing that again."

"Oh, my god," I laugh as I crouch by his side, offering him

a hand up. He grabs my forearm and groans, and I easily lift him to his feet. "I'll teach you to drive the golf cart soon, okay?"

Ronan's eyebrows shoot to his hairline. "Are you *sure* about that offer?"

I squint at him. "Should I be?"

"Yes. I'm definitely a world-class driver. I've never had any incidents."

I hesitate and glance out the large front window to the driveway. "I mean… I'm not at the top of the golf cart hierarchy yet. What's the worst that could happen?"

"We'll find out." Ronan sighs and sits on top of a cardboard box, which immediately buckles under his weight. He just sticks out his legs and rides it down until he reaches the contents and stops sinking.

I can't help laughing as I sit on the arm of the sofa next to him, and he leans the side of his head against my knee. "What's wrong?" I ask him, gazing down at the top of his head. It's all I can do to resist stroking his hair, because if I do that…

My self-control will crumble.

Instead, I gently rest my hand on his shoulder. "Is this your schoolwork or something?"

Ronan shakes his head. "Not even. I did something dumb. Maybe smart, but really dumb." He looks up at me.

My breath catches in my chest. Even with his sweaty cheeks and tangled blond hair, he's… angelic. I can't stop looking at him. I bite my tongue and wait, praying that I come off more cool and calm than my heartbeat is right now.

"I asked Professor Meyer what I should do to improve my technical skills. And now I have…" he waves a hand at the row of cardboard boxes. "My first official job in the industry."

"Whoa." I squeeze Ronan's shoulder and grin at him. "Congratulations!"

He doesn't look as excited as I might have thought. "Professor Meyer told them I can start right away as long as it wraps up in November, so it won't interfere with my showcase."

That sounds even better to me. "So what is it?" I ask, shaking my head. "And why does it take up half the living room?"

"Piecework. Grunt work, basically," Ronan explains before I have to ask. "For an outdoor gear company. Exactly what my parents were afraid of me doing. But... I guess it's better if I'm choosing to do it?"

I lightly run my hand from his shoulder to the back of his neck, and then I rub gentle circles with my thumb. "I'm proud of you. That was a great idea, asking her what you need to do. She wouldn't have hooked you up with them if she didn't think you'd learn, right?"

Ronan doesn't hesitate. "No. You're right."

"And she wouldn't have recommended you to them if she didn't think you were good enough."

Ronan actually stops and stares at me. "Oh," he says at last. "I hadn't thought of that." But he's still not quite as happy as I might have thought. He's watching me warily, and I have the feeling I know what that look is.

He thinks he's about to disappoint me.

"So, what's the catch?"

Ronan swallows hard and looks across the living room to the bookshelf, now filled with his books and magazines and art supplies. "I'm already starting from scratch on the biggest project of the semester. And now I'll be working. I'm not going to have time to do *anything* but study, work, sleep…"

Now I see where this is going.

Ronan's lips curl even further down as he gazes sadly up at me. "I'm not going to have enough time with you."

He's the sweetest thing I've ever seen.

"Oh, Ronan," I murmur, leaning down to wrap my arms around his shoulders and hug him from behind. "There's never enough time with you. I accepted that from the beginning." When I let go of him, I scoot over onto the couch and nudge him to join me.

"No, but…" Ronan sits next to me, curling his legs up under himself. Both his hands rest on one of my thighs as he gazes anxiously up at me. "After last weekend, I just… I don't want to ghost you."

I chuckle. "We're living together," I point out, as gently as I can, though I don't think that's what he's really worried about. "And I'm not going anywhere, either."

Ronan quickly glances down at his hands, drumming his fingers lightly on my legs. Then he slides one hand up my thigh toward my crotch, peeking up through his lashes at me.

His touch never fails to make my skin light up. Goosebumps race along my forearms, and my heartbeat speeds up.

But Ronan isn't… for lack of a better word, *sparkling.*

I press my hand on top of his, stopping him. When he looks up at me, I just tilt my head and ask the question with my eyes.

What are you doing?

He licks his lips nervously. "It won't be crazy busy all the time," he tells me softly, like he's trying to negotiate with me, and he thinks I have the upper hand.

Okay. I'm stopping this, now.

"Ronan," I tell him, my voice sharp. He quickly looks up at me, and the spark of fear in his eyes makes me wince. I squeeze his hand gently and soften my tone. "This isn't... I don't want to be friends with benefits."

He pauses and watches me closely, his eyes flickering between mine. "Why not?"

"I want more," I tell him firmly. "And I don't want to rush into it. If I have to wait until the end of the semester, so what? Like I said, neither of us is going anywhere."

Ronan just shakes his head a little. "Why?" he asks, frustration in his voice. "How can you... how do you know you'll feel the same way in a couple of months?"

"I can't," I admit. "But this is how we find out, right?"

Ronan sighs, and his hand finally relaxes under mine. "A couple of months seems like a lifetime."

"I want something that lasts a lot longer than that." I smile at him softly when he glances up at me with those startled eyes. "I'm willing to wait."

Ronan hesitates. "I... I don't want to sound like a dick," he starts, and I grin at him to welcome whatever he's going to say. He blushes. "This isn't... like you and your ex, is it?"

I blink at him. Not because I'm mad, but because I don't get it.

Ronan finally huffs out a little sigh. "You're the kindest man I've ever met. I don't want to use that kindness. It would make me feel just as rotten as... as you feeling like you're distracting me. You know?"

I snort. "If you're being honest about your intentions, it's not using me. And you've been honest about *all* your intentions since day one."

At last, Ronan giggles for real. "Yeah. I have been," he admits. "Maybe too honest."

"No such thing," I promise him.

It's a beautiful moment, watching the hope return to Ronan's eyes. He turns all shy, and then his cheeks flush pink.

And it makes it *so* much harder to keep my hands to myself.

"You trust yourself so much," Ronan says at last. "I like that about you."

"I trust my gut more than anything. And I've wanted you ever since I saw you, too." I wink at him. "Not just in bed, although that part is… life-changing."

Ronan laughs richly. He tilts head back and making a gesture like a movie poster. "Ronan Ashfield: life-changing in bed."

I laugh, too, and then I gently nudge him with my knee. "I think we could be great boyfriends. That's all I'm saying."

"*Oh.*" Ronan beams at me, and there it is—that sparkle again, through and through. "So it's like a boyfriend betrothal."

"A…"

He goes bright red. "Forget I said that."

"Not a chance. I'm never forgetting it."

"Oh, god." Ronan covers his face with both hands. "Kill me now."

"Never. In fact, I'm here to protect you from all those serial killers… my betrothed," I grin.

Ronan heaves a sigh that makes me snort with laughter. "*Anyway,*" he says, dragging his palms down his face as he looks at me. He raises one hand to cup my cheek with a little, wistful sigh. "It's going to be hard to keep my hands off you. You're sure we really can't just…? You know?"

"Sleep together now, figure out our feelings later?" He nods, and I grin. "When has that ever worked?"

"No. You're right," Ronan finally says. He pulls his knees up to his chest and wraps his arms around them, resting his chin on his knees to study me.

For once, I can't tell what's going through his head.

"What?" I finally ask him softly.

"I just… I've never had someone believe in me like this." Ronan clears his throat. "You believe in who I'm going to be. And you're not asking me to make compromises first. In fact…" He squints at me. "…you get kind of mad at me when I do."

That all sounds right.

"Okay," Ronan murmurs at last. He drops his knees and curls them up by his side again as he looks up at me—and smiles with all that sparkling hope that makes my soul sing.

His eyes drop to my lips and linger, and I pause.

Should I?

Fuck it. I don't want to let being careful get in the way of what I want.

So I cup Ronan's cheeks gently between my palms, and I lean in to cross the distance between us… and I press our lips together, nice and long and slow. The air whooshes out of his lungs, and his shoulders slowly drop, and I keep on kissing him until all the tension is gone.

I back up every word of my promises with that kiss—and I take what I need, too.

A glimpse at the future that's so worth waiting for.

Then I pull away, and Ronan catches my hands. One at a time, he bows his head to kiss each of my palms. Then he lets go and smiles. "I'd better open these boxes."

"Then I won't get in your way." I smile as I get up. "Coming downstairs for dinner tonight?"

"Yeah. I'd love that." Ronan smiles up at me with shining eyes. "Thank you."

I wink at him as I head downstairs. "Bring your appetite," I call out, and then I whistle my way down the stairs.

I know what I want. And finally, it's something worth waiting for.

CHAPTER

Twenty

RONAN

My mind is in a hundred places as I stumble out of the shower. I haven't finished this week's assignment, and I've only got a few hours before I have to leave for my ferry.

"God," I cover my yawn as I grope around to find the doorway to the master bedroom. A few weeks into the new routine, I'm just about used to it—even sleeping in here.

Not that I get much sleep these days.

I was up late again last night, and all for an optional project that I won't even get credit for in class.

It was another one of Professor Meyer's off-handed suggestions, slipped in between her Powerpoint slides like an afterthought.

Now that you know how to do a portfolio critique, you might do it to your own portfolio someday. Treat it like someone else's work and critique it the same way. Notice what you'd do differently now.

These days, I pay attention to everything she says.

She was right about this new job, after all. I'm getting better at everything I've been avoiding for three years... and without the pressure of designing, I'm finally learning to take pride in my work.

Another yawn hits me like a truck as I rummage around for a shirt and a pair of jeans. I finish off the day's outfit with a cute sweater, because autumn is well and truly here.

And it's gotta be cute, just in case Alph comes upstairs.

When I get to the kitchen table, where my sewing machine now lives, I stop short. I smell coffee.

No, I *see* coffee—a mug of it sitting right by my sewing machine. And there's a plate with a breakfast bagel.

Just the way I like it: overloaded with scrambled eggs and bacon, dripping with butter... and I even spot the bright green flash of an avocado slice poking out.

"Alph," I breathe out as I pick up my coffee.

I'm suddenly grinning, almost forgetting all about the stress awaiting me today—and every day, for weeks to come.

Gravel crunches on the driveway. I head to the front window, where I can watch Alph backing up the golf cart to the road. He hops out to close the driveway gate, and my grin gets even bigger.

He's dressed for work, in his old sailor jeans and his tight little ferry sweater, with a rain jacket tied around his shoulders. He's walking with that particular rolling gait that's always accompanied by a cheerful whistle.

I pull the curtains open, waving an arm over my head to catch Alph's attention. He stops next to the golf cart and looks up at me, shielding his eyes. He's got that *everything okay?* look on his face.

Before he can come back inside, though, I just smile and wave at him, holding up the coffee mug.

Alph grins back at me. He raises one hand to his lips to blow a kiss at me.

Oh my god.

My heart is melting. I giggle and pretend to catch it, carefully pressing it to my cheek. Then I blow a kiss right back at him.

Alph's head snaps back. He watches the invisible kiss like a baseball flying toward him, jogging backward.

I'm laughing in great big snorts now, hastily setting the mug on the windowsill so I don't spill coffee everywhere. "What a dork."

Alph finally leaps for it, just manages to catch it, and wipes a hand across his forehead before tucking my kiss safely in his breast pocket. Then he winks and jogs forward to get into the golf cart, and he's off for the day.

I breathe out a sigh as I let the curtain fall back into place, bringing my coffee back to the machine.

I've been surprised how good this feels. I thought it would ache 24/7… but it's been the opposite. It's not like we're an ocean apart—just one flight of stairs.

Just last night when I was working late, Alph came upstairs and sat quietly in the corner armchair to read. He didn't say a word, just kept me company as I worked, and it made my heart soar.

And he kissed me good night.

I'm grinning stupidly again, pressing the tips of my fingers against my lips to recall the taste and the gentle warmth of his mouth.

"Okay," I say out loud. Hot bagel in hand, it's time to face my sewing machine and start my day.

No more compromising, no more offering up only the parts of myself that I think I can persuade someone to want. Alph's willing to wait… as long as I give him all I've got.

And at long last, that's exactly what I'm doing.

Twenty~One

ALPH

"Take it slow in the corners, Ronan. Slower than that. Slower—!" Too late. I grab the bar behind our heads, shifting my weight toward the centre of the golf cart. "Whoa…!"

It's nothing compared to Ronan's screech. "Eeeeeyaaaa—"

We hurtle around the corner, gravel flies… and we make it.

Ronan takes his foot off the gas. He's still clutching the steering wheel for dear life as we slow to a rolling halt. "Oops."

"Phew," I breathe out, letting go of the bar to clutch my chest instead. "Hey, it's okay. We're still on four wheels. You're getting better… on the whole."

Problem is, the more confident Ronan is, the faster he wants to go. It's very on-brand of him.

Ronan ducks his head sheepishly. "Yeah. Maybe you should drive?"

I just shake my head. We're just around the corner from the wharf, where he's catching the ferry to class, and my brothers and I are meeting at the coffee shop to catch up on life.

Which I'm pretty sure means grilling me about Ronan. I can't help but notice that all of them are conveniently available, even though it's a weekday morning.

"No," I tell him. "I believe in you. Keep going."

How fitting.

I have my own selfish reasons for saying that. If Ronan doesn't practice, he'll never get better. And I want him to see that he *can* haul his own stuff on and off Sunrise Island. Otherwise, this *will* just be an artist's retreat—not a practical, long-term home.

A home with me.

Ronan looks up at me with a little smile, and then it slowly becomes a grin. "Okay."

He turns back to the road and accelerates again, quiet and focused this time. He sticks to the speed limit and avoids all the potholes for the rest of the short journey.

Finally, he squeezes the golf cart into a spot all by himself, and I can't stop myself from beaming with pride.

"I did it!" Ronan turns off the ignition and beams up at me, flinging himself off the cart to pirouette behind it. "That was my best trip!"

"It was." I clamber to solid ground, laughing quietly at how pleased he is. "Really good—mmph!"

Ronan flings himself at me, wraps his arms around my shoulders, and kisses me. His mouth slides across mine, hot and quick with adrenaline, sending *all* my blood rushing down south.

Holy shit.

We pull apart with a gasp, and I lick my lips slowly as I study his flushed cheeks and wide eyes.

For a moment, neither of us know what to do. Then a honk nearby startles us both.

It's the two-minute warning for the ferry.

"Oh shit. Gotta go!" Ronan grabs his backpack and all the bags from the back of the golf cart.

I lean over to pull the keys out of the ignition, waving them at him. "Don't forget these."

"Oh! Sorry," Ronan gasps. He obviously thinks I'm scolding him for leaving them there. I wait patiently, jangling them at him, and he blinks. "Wait. Do you mean…?"

I shrug. "I can walk home. You're the one with all the stuff."

Ronan beams at me, freeing up a hand to take them and tuck them carefully into his pocket. "Thank you," he murmurs. Then he gasps, remembering his sense of urgency and scurrying for the dock. "Bye!"

I wave at the all-too-familiar sight of his retreating back, smiling as I watch him go.

A wolf-whistle nearby catches my attention. When I look over at the coffee shop, I see a bunch of familiar faces all at once.

Oh. I'm the last one here. And they're all grinning like they saw everything that just went down.

"Well, well, well." Carter holds out a coffee cup to me and claps his arm around my shoulders in a hug. I hug the rest of them, too—Zach, Drew, Murph.

Last but not least is Felix. My little brother doesn't say a word, but he's glowing as he wraps me up in a tight hug.

We'd take over the whole coffee shop if we tried to sit inside, so we set off to the sleep slope down to the beach. The nearby sound of the ferry engine tells me that Ronan made it just in time.

"Guess that boyfriend betrothal is going well, huh?" Carter grins.

"Yeah. Really well." I settle down on a smooth driftwood log by the shoreline. A few of the guys sit on it, and others perch on the rocks and boulders nearby.

We're overlooking the harbour, and I can't stop myself from trying to steal a glimpse of Ronan on board the retreating ferry.

"Has it been hard waiting for him?" Felix asks. He draws his leg up to sit sideways, watching me carefully. "When we got together…" he gestures toward Carter, then grins as I wrinkle my nose. "Well, I can't imagine waiting. That's all."

At least they got straight to the point.

"Mmm," I hum, feeling everyone's eyes on me as I look toward the ferry again. "It's not always easy. But it's better than the way I just rushed into things before. This time…" I shake my head. "We get to learn all about each other first."

"That actually sounds sweet," Zach murmured.

"It is." I'm smiling again. I can't help myself. "Everything I learn about him just makes me like him more."

There's a few moments of silence as they trade glances.

"I was worried at first," Carter finally says. "But, you know what? I think it's been good for you."

The others nod with agreement. "Yeah?" I ask, tearing my eyes off the ferry at last to glance at my friends.

It's Murph, the quietest one of our group, who answers. "You're more chill."

"At first, I thought you'd rearrange your life around Ronan's," Drew says, carefully. "Making sure you're always home when he is. Doing everything he needs done."

"You've done that before," Carter says, clapping my shoulder gently. "But this is *here*. It would be a lot worse."

In my own home, where I can't just up and leave... I could start to feel like a stranger.

The breath rushes out of my lungs as I see what they mean.

"I might have done that once," I admit. "But not anymore. I'm putting my love life on hold for him, because he's worth it." I smile, peeling back the coffee cup lid for a sip.

The more I get to know Ronan, the more I can't imagine wanting anyone else.

"But I'm not putting my whole life on hold," I add, looking around at them. "I promise."

Carter grins and clasps my arm, while the others nod and murmur their agreement.

My little brother is beaming at me the hardest of all.

"Yeah?" I murmur to Felix.

He blinks away the tears shimmering in his eyes and squints over the harbour. "I'm just glad, that's all. You've spent your life looking after me. It's about time you look after you."

I reach out for a fist bump, but what I get is a hug—and coffee very nearly spilled over my leg. I yelp, pulling away just in time as everyone hisses and then laughs with relief.

I settle back down and clear my throat. "Actually, while we're on that subject... I've been reading up lately." I can't blame them for their surprised looks—I've always been better with my hands than with words. "Ronan said something that gave me an idea. And I can't stop thinking about it."

"Spit it out," Carter kicks me in the shin.

"Okay, okay. I want to become a tour guide." I'm half-expecting them to scoff at me. This part of the world is known for the great outdoors. Tour operators are dime-a-dozen. "But boat tours, right? Talking about Sunrise Island. Nobody else is doing that. We could do short trips at first, in between the hourly ferry runs."

When I finally stop for a breath, Zach claps and whoops. Drew pumps his fist in the air. Felix is bouncing up and down and grinning. Even Murph gives me a slow, approving nod.

"You think I should do it?" I ask, blinking at them.

What about all the things that could go wrong?

"Remember when we were kids?" Felix grins. "You used to do pretend tours for us. Half the facts were made up, but that made it more fun."

I crack up with laughter. I can't believe I'd forgotten that.

"For *years*, I believed the lighthouse was built by a special species of ant found only here," Zach grumbles, and we all burst out laughing.

The conversation finally moves on, but I can't stop smiling.

Ronan didn't just give me the idea. He's shown me what happens when I pay attention to what I want—without settling for anything less.

I just hope I can make him proud.

CHAPTER

Twenty-Two

RONAN

It's crunch time.

The showcase is breathing down my neck, and there's no more avoiding it.

I've finished all my other assignments, and I've wrapped up the gig Professor Meyer recommended me for. When I delivered the last box of hiking trousers to them, they told me I'd be welcome back anytime.

I'm proud of myself for doing so well... but I hope I don't have to take them up on it. I'm on the way to my first one-on-one evaluation with Professor Meyer, so I guess I'm about to find out.

"Hands and arms inside the boat, folks!" Alph cheerfully calls over the intercom. "Don't hold us responsible for stray feet, either."

He shuts the ferry engine off and walks to the side of the boat, lassoing the first cleat as we gently bump up against the harbour wharf.

I get up, but I hang back to let everyone else off first.

When I finally approach, Alph turns and smiles brightly at me.

"There's my best-behaved passenger. Got your portfolio?" he asks, for the tenth time, even though I'm clutching it tight against my chest. "Got your winning smile? Ah, there it is."

I giggle and blush, swatting him gently with my portfolio. "I've got it all."

Alph smiles back at me. "You really do," he tells me with such sincerity that I stand up a little bit straighter. "Now, got your coffee and your snacks?"

"All of it," I groan, laughing. "I have it all. I promise."

"Okay, good. Just checking. Go kill it, Ronan."

"Thanks," I whisper, stretching onto tiptoe to kiss Alph's cheek. Then I scramble off the ferry to the dock, beaming away to myself.

A few steps away, I turn back to look at him, and I can't help stopping. He's still just standing there, one hand on the side of the boat, smiling at me with so much pride.

My eyes are suddenly wet, and my chest is glowing with warmth.

I'm so goddamn lucky.

I wish I could plan something for him to look forward to —besides the end of this chaotic whirlwind. Something to show him that I'll always make room for him.

That he'll never have to wait for me again.

"What?" Alph frowns when he notices me stopping. "You didn't forget anything?"

"No, no." I clear my throat. "I just had an idea. Can you ask Kieran to reserve a table at the restaurant?"

"Reserve?" Alph asks, tilting his head.

I don't even know if they take reservations, but I press on. "Yeah. For lunch, on showcase day."

Alph looks even more puzzled. "Sure, sure. Yeah. How many people?"

He doesn't get it yet.

A blush rises in my cheeks as I smile at him, just studying him. He looks so natural here, like this is where he belongs. His hair wafts in the ocean breeze, and his jaw reminds me of the sleek cut of the boat's wake in a crystal-calm ocean.

Finally, Alph's eyes widen. "Oh." He rubs the back of his neck. "For two?"

"Yeah. Two."

Alph grins and salutes at me, standing up a little straighter. "Okiedokie. I'll do that straight away."

I flutter my fingers in a wave as I trot through the little waiting room and up to the wharf ramp that leads to the sidewalk.

From here, it's a long walk or a short bus ride. But it's a beautiful day, and I suddenly have a lot of excitement to burn off before I can focus on what I'm going to say to Professor Meyer. Maybe I should walk?

"Hey," a familiar voice snaps.

Someone steps in front of me, blocking the way off the ramp, and I jump backward. I skid on the metal, but I grab the rail in time to steady myself.

It's Derek. He's got one hand on each railing, and he's sneering down at me.

Keeping my eyes fixed on him, I slowly let go of the railing and wrap both arms around my portfolio again so it's tight against my chest.

"You think there's anything in there worth holding onto?" Derek laughs in his meanest voice. He moves toward me all of a sudden, pushing with both hands, and I flinch backward and hold on even tighter.

He was just feinting. He laughs cruelly at me, takes another step closer, and then another.

"Just quit," Derek tells me. "Before I make you quit."

I lift my chin, stare him right in the eye… and I plant my feet.

"No."

Derek stops, too. He snorts at me, lifting his lip. "She's gonna laugh you right out of the room." He reaches out, taking a swipe at my portfolio, and I twist my body aside so he misses. "Give that here!"

"Maybe she will," I tell him, keeping my voice cool but raising it to match his. "Or maybe not. I'll let her make that decision, because your opinion is worth *nothing*. On the rubric, or to me."

My head spins as I take a deep breath, smiling at the salty seaweed tang that I've grown so used to.

That feels good. *Really* good.

Derek's jaw drops. "Listen here, twerp—"

"No," I snap back at him, and he stops like he's shocked I'd even say anything back to him. "This isn't high school. It's the real world. Obviously we don't like each other." I shrug. "So what? We can be fuckings adults about it. We don't just threaten to beat each other up—"

"Hey!"

The holler behind me makes Derek almost jumps out of his skin, but I just grin. That's all it takes for me to recognize Alph.

That, and the footsteps storming up the metal ramp.

"If you don't get away from him right now, I'm gonna break your nose."

Oh, my god.

I lean on the railing all of a sudden, my knees going weak.

My message might be slightly undermined, but I can't really bring myself to feel annoyed about it.

Not when I want to swoon right off this ramp.

"Fuck off," Derek snarls, but he turns tail and hurries off—about as fast as it's possible to go without actually running. Even at the top of the ramp, when he gets to the sidewalk, he runs flat into several people in his haste to escape.

I turn to Alph with a grin, but he's already sweeping me up in his arms, hugging me so tightly against him that all the air rushes out of my lungs.

"Did he rattle you? Are you okay? He didn't hurt you, did he?"

"I'm fine," I squeak, finally managing to interrupt Alph as I tap his chest.

He loosens his hold, taking me by the shoulders. "Okay," he breathes out. "You're sure?"

"Really." I giggle softly. "Just… overcome."

"Overcome?" He looks worried. "How?"

"In my loins," I grin dizzily at him. "Like a maiden rescued from the dragon by her fair knight?"

Alph's lips slowly part. He clears his throat.

"Anyway, isn't your ferry late now?"

"Nobody was here yet," Alph shakes his head. "And even if they were, it's always worth a diversion for you."

I beam up at him, and then I wink and sidle closer. "So. About that overcoming…"

Alph's cheeks flush deep red. He clears his throat and hastily straightens his jacket. "Well, I… I should, er. Get back to the ferry. You know."

I know, I know. Now that I've reminded him he's sailing late, he's going to worry about it.

"But not before you claim a gallant hero's reward, right?"

Alph stops and stares at me. I bat my lashes at him, and I can actually see the moment his resolve gives in.

He grunts and strides up to me, grabbing me by the hips and hauling me against him. Then he crushes a kiss against my lips and our mouths clash, hot and furious and fast.

"Nnnh!" I whimper. Sparks fly across every inch of my skin. Within seconds, I'm throbbing hard, aching against my jeans. I press closer, and instead of pulling back, his kiss deepens. He shoves his tongue into my mouth like he's trying to claim me—and leave a warning to all who come near me.

He slides his hand to the back of my head and tightens his fingers into a fist, tugging at my hair… reminding me of our one perfect night together, and all those nights yet to come.

At last, Alph lets go. I stare up at him, open-mouthed and staggered, as he winks and raises his hand in a wave.

Somehow, when I wasn't paying attention, he learned to keep up with me… and then some.

"Keep your eyes on the prize," Alph tells me, his eyes glittering. "I know I am."

The showcase. Focus on the showcase.

I giggle and nod breathlessly, turning and trotting up the ramp.

When I'm at the top, another thought occurs to me, and I stop and turn to him, but he's already disappeared around the corner and into the ferry waiting room.

Alph meant that *I'm* the prize!

That's one decision made. I'm going to walk up to the campus… with a spring in my step.

CHAPTER
Twenty~Three

ALPH

THE EVENING BEFORE THE SHOWCASE, RONAN'S LIST OF THINGS to freak out about is probably a mile long.

It's not just that I can't help because I don't have the know-how. Much more importantly, I won't—because I know Ronan's got this.

He doesn't need me jumping in to rescue him when he's not drowning.

I'm trying my best to stay hands-off. The last time I went upstairs was to bring Ronan lunch. I persuaded him to eat a few bites of his sandwich before he panicked about the crumbs and told me to leave the plate in the kitchen.

I bet you anything it's still there.

But now… I'm getting really worried.

The noise upstairs has been at a fever pitch all day long. Loud rock music, hammering, sewing, furious pacing and phone calls, and a whole lot of swearing—and that was all before 9am.

Now, it's eerily quiet.

I poke my head through the open door at the bottom of

the stairs and wait for a few moments, half-expecting to be startled by another explosion of sound... but there's still nothing.

"Ronan?" I murmur, carefully making my way up the stairs. "Are you here?" I haven't heard the golf cart leave, so I'm starting to wonder if he snuck out the back door.

Still nothing.

"Are you running away from home to live in the woods? Felix tried that once, you know. I freaked out, but Mom just baked brownies. He was back within the hour."

The cardboard boxes of piecework are gone, but I still can't see through the banisters. They've been replaced by a row of magnetic whiteboards, each with numbers and words I've stopped trying to understand.

I poke my head around the top of the staircase.

There he is—lying face-down on a pile of fabrics on the couch, his blond hair splayed every which way.

"You okay?"

Ronan doesn't even move. He just moans quietly.

"It's like that again, huh?" I pick my way through the clutter until I can crouch by the sofa.

I can't say I'm surprised. There's a reason I asked Berty for the morning shift today... and then the whole weekend off.

"There's a lasagna in the oven," I tell Ronan. I sit cross-legged on the floor, reaching out to stroke his hair. "And I'm going to make you come eat it when it's done. And I'm also going to force coffee on you every hour, unless you say otherwise."

Ronan finally turns his head enough that he can peer at me with one eye. "Yes, please. Sorry about the disaster zone in your very nice home," he mumbles against the cushions. "I'm a raccoon in a trash can."

I laugh, finger-combing the hair back and out of Ronan's eyes. "It's okay. I know it all makes sense to you."

Ronan moans. "Not anymore. It's just chaos. Everything is chaos."

"Come on." I stand up and bend over, wriggling my hands and forearms underneath Ronan until I can shift him out of the way. Then I sit down and pull his head into my lap. "Look at me, sweetheart."

Ronan rolls all the way over until he's on his other side, knees curled up by his chest, peering up at me.

My poor angel. He looks like a robot who's run out of battery.

"I'm proud of you. Always. Okay?"

Ronan covers his face with his hands. "You've been waiting for me for so long."

I shake my head. Every night, I call up the memory of Ronan's warm, smooth skin against mine, pressing my nose into his freshly-shampooed hair, listening to his breathing turn steady and deep.

"It's not like the dinosaurs came and went since… you know, we came and stayed."

Ronan has to take a moment to think about that. Then he cracks up, snorts in a tiny little giggle. "Was that a dirty joke?"

"It might have been. Maybe you've been rubbing off on me this whole time," I raise my eyebrows.

"Not *nearly* as much as I've wanted to."

"Me, too." The hunger is impossible to ignore when I'm stroking Ronan's hair, running my hands down his shoulders and arms. My voice crackles with it, hoarse and raw.

Ronan's eyes widen as he looks up at me. Then he groans. "I just can't stop thinking…"

"Mmhmm?"

Whatever the dirty fantasy, I don't think we have time for it. But I'll humour him and let him say it.

"What if you've waited… given up all this time with me… and they boo me?" Ronan's hands slide down to curl up on his chest as he watches me, looking stricken with worry.

I stare at him for a few moments, and then I press my palm over both of his hands. "Then I'll be even prouder of you," I tell him firmly. "Because then you've done something that blew their minds so much they couldn't handle it." I whistle under my breath. "Imagine. That would be incredible."

"Oh," Ronan breathes out. "Oh, yeah."

"Hell, you could walk out there to dead silence, and you'd still be worth waiting for." I frown down at him, and then I gently shake his hands against his chest. "Because I'm *not* out here wringing my hands, waiting for a crumb of your time. I have a little more self-respect than that."

"No. I know. I didn't mean…" Ronan trails off. "What *are* you waiting for?"

I smile. "I'm waiting for you to be ready to give me *all* of you. Especially the part that scares you right now."

Ronan slowly sits up and turns to look at me, one hand rising to his chest. The other hand is still clutching mine, so I slip my fingers between his.

"That part you're afraid they won't like—or I won't like? I promise you… I already like it. And the rest of the world can damn well take it or leave it."

Ronan's smile is back, even though his eyes are wet with tears. "I…" he trails off.

Then, he just flings his arms around me and kisses me. It's a kiss that builds and builds, quick as a wildfire and hotter still, until my desire is so thick and dizzying that I can't think straight.

I want him to know that he's mine—every part of him, in every moment. I want to steal him away from the world... but I know he has something he needs to say to the world first.

Ronan's the first one to pull away, fire gleaming in his eyes. "I'm going to finish tonight," he promises me. "We *will* have that romantic lunch. And I'm not going to say one word about the showcase, or school, or my stupid ex-roommates, or... or any of this."

I don't doubt him on the first two points.

But that last one...

My lips twitch as I try to hide my smile. I can't imagine Ronan stifling one moment of his excitement and nervousness and pride, and even the vindication that's driven him to improve so much, so quickly. And if it makes him happy, I would never want him to.

"Just you and me, at last," Ronan promises fervently.

I chuckle softly, pressing a kiss on his lips. "It's been you and me all along."

Then, I finally push myself to my feet. Ronan reaches out for my hand and I take it to pull him up, too.

"Whew," he sighs, shaking his head and looking at his whiteboards.

I squeeze his shoulder. "How about that coffee?"

"Give it to me, Alph," Ronan grins. He sounds tired, but the fight is finally back in his voice. "As often as you want."

"Ohhh, yes," I promise, swallowing the shiver of delight as he flicks a look up at me through his lashes. "Believe me... I plan to."

Twenty~Four

RONAN

I'M FULL, HAPPY, AND TOTALLY SMITTEN.

I don't even mind that Kieran's way of reserving a table was to swap out the basket of condiments for a vase of fresh roses and a scrap of paper that reads, *RESERVED: LOVERS*.

It made for a nice backdrop in my update selfie, sent to my classmates' WhatsApp group chat the minute we arrived. I *had* to—after all, I've spent the last three weeks talking their ears off about this date.

"My phone is going to blow up when I turn it back on…" I trail off, blushing. I glance sheepishly at Alph across the half-eaten dessert brownie. "Oops. In fairness, I didn't *say* it was about the showcase."

I'm amazed I've made it this long without breaking any of my conversation rules. It was inevitable I'd slip up sooner or later.

Alph just grins. "It's okay. Besides, we don't have long before we have to go, so—"

"Shit. What?"

I press and hold the button on my phone. I'm too impatient to wait for it to turn on, so I grab Alph's wrist, trying to look at his watch upside-down.

For weeks, Professor Meyer has made it clear that setup is at 3:30, and not a minute later. This is the one day that not even the Terrible Trio will get away with sauntering in late.

"It's a quarter to two," Alph tells me, smiling. "Relax. I've been keeping an eye out."

"Oh my god," I sigh, clutching my chest. "You scared me. Aren't we taking the three o'clock ferry?"

"Sorry, sorry." Alph holds up his hands and laugh. "I was just thinking we could do the ferry at two instead…" he trails off as my phone buzzes like it's trying to leap into the ocean.

Mostly notifications from our WhatsApp class group, ranging from good luck wishes to blind panic, and offers of help once we get to the venue. And, of course, reactions to the photo of me and Alph, with the roses prominently in the background.

No messages at all from any of my ex-roomies. They couldn't make it more obvious that they think they're above the rest of us.

Dickheads.

When I squint at Alph, he's still waiting for my answer… and he definitely looks like he's up to something. "An hour early? Why?"

Alph widens his eyes and tries to look innocent, which just makes him look ten times as adorable but half as inno-cent. "Just in case?"

"In case of a traffic jam… between here and the harbourfront theatre right there?" I point at it across the water, and Alph looks even guiltier. Finally, I relent with a laugh. "Okay. But they probably won't let us in. And I'll have my suitcases."

"That's why I'm taking you to the coffee shop next door."

I *could* use more coffee before tonight…

It must have been three in the morning by the time everything was packed into my two big, yellow suitcases.

"Okay," I agree, standing up. "Let's pay."

Alph scoffs and waves a hand. "Already done," he tells me, even though he hasn't stood up from the table. I assume he's talked to Kieran in advance. I even have suspicions that the roses are his doing, too… but I won't call him out on it.

He really is being the world's greatest boyfriend. Or… boyfriend-to-be.

"Thank you," I tell him, and we slip out before anyone can see us and try to start a conversation.

For now, I still want it to be just him and me.

Knowing that Alph was dozing off in my bed last night, just waiting for me to join him—it lit a hell of a fire under my ass.

By the time I joined him, I barely remember closing my eyes. I woke up to breakfast in bed, and then we cuddled for a while as I made mental checklist.

If this is what our future together will be like? I can't freaking wait.

There's only one thing left to do: head home to grab my packed suitcases, and then get back in time for the ferry.

"Aren't we pushing it a little close?"

Alph starts up the golf cart with a grin. "I'm a fast driver," he promises. "Let's go!"

The whole way home, I'm beaming to myself, because I'm starting to believe this is possible.

I can really be myself, get the boyfriend, *and* get the dream job. If all goes well tonight, of course… but I believe in myself these days, too.

As we pull around the final corner and speed toward the house, Alph grins breathlessly. "Sorry it's such a rush. I just didn't want to interrupt you while you were looking so cute."

"It's okay. If we *don't* make it back to the ferry on time, you bring me straight back here and spend that hour making it up to me," I tell him, boldly lifting my chin.

Alph swallows hard and tears his gaze off me to focus on the road. His nostrils flare, and he shifts against the bench a little bit as I grin.

As he arrives, I lean in and whisper, "In every… possible… way."

Then we both hop off, sprinting for the porch stairs.

I beat him there, fumbling for my keys to unlock it.

"It would have been faster going in the back," Alph murmurs.

I giggle. "I want you to remember that for later." Finally, I dig out the key from my inside pocket to unlock the door.

I take the stairs two at a time… and then I skid to a halt.

"Ronan," Alph hisses from the front landing. "Ronan, stop!"

I already know what he's trying to say. My brain is screaming it at me: *something's wrong.*

I skid to a halt and stare, half-aware of Alph rushing downstairs.

It's too cold in here.

And the living room mess isn't the same as I left it last night.

My sewing machine is on the floor, smashed into pieces. The white boards are face-down, and the drawings I carefully Blu-tacked onto the wall… ripped into shreds.

"What the—" I clap a hand over my mouth as I slowly back up, staring at the carnage.

But it gets so much worse.

My two bright yellow suitcases were carefully packed with my whole semester's work—everything I need for the runway showcase tonight. When we left for the restaurant, they were sitting right here.

And they're gone.

"Alph!" I scream, sprinting down the stairs. I fling myself around the corner of the landing to the second flight of stairs, and straight into the middle of his apartment.

He's just standing there with his jaw hanging open, staring at his front door.

It's wide open.

I plop my ass heavily on the stairs, dropping my head into my hands.

That's it, then.

Now I know how—and I'd be willing to stake my life on *who* took my stuff. But with no idea where they are now, I don't have a snowflake's chance in hell of getting those suitcases back.

Tonight, or at all.

I wipe my hands down my face as I look up. "Alph," I whisper through numb lips.

Alph slowly turns to look at me. The guilt is already written all over his face.

I don't want to... but I have to ask.

"Did you lock your door?"

Alph doesn't say a word. He just bows his head. And, like that, my world shakes itself apart.

CHAPTER
Twenty-Five

RONAN

I SHOULDN'T HAVE TRUSTED ANYONE.

Because it isn't just trusting one person to keep you safe, is it? It ends up meaning I have to trust everyone that *he* trusts. And if he can't say no to the whole damn world…

What's left for me?

Alph slides the door closed.

"I'll fix this, Ronan," he says. The words ring hollow in my ears when I can't see how, but he sounds determined. "I swear I will."

"How?" I peek up through my fingers, then slowly rake my nails across my scalp to try to calm down. "They could be anywhere."

It's got to be my ex-roommates. They've been spiralling all semester, skipping assignments and portfolio reviews. And I can't get Derek's threats out of my head. But even if I head straight to the showcase, I'll need evidence.

I've been doing the right thing: keeping my head down, working hard, and ignoring them. I wanted to win this fair and square—or at least beat the three of them.

I should take it as a compliment. They're scared to hell that I'll beat them for the top spot—and the XX Gracieux job.

But I'm furious, and worse still, helpless.

"Remember what I told you that first day?" Alph strides back over and grabs me by the arm. He hauls me to the feet, dusts me off, and ushers me up the stairs. "This is an island. Nobody gets on or off without being seen."

I want to have hope. After all, I don't think any of my ex-roomies are criminal masterminds. They have to be heading for the mainland—and if they aren't, Alph knows every hiding spot on this island.

"Come on," Alph says, slamming the door closed behind us as we scramble down to the driveway. "Hold on tight."

He's not kidding about that.

Alph peels out of the driveway and around the corner with the focus of as a race car driver. He floors it down the road, and the only time he slows down is when we see people walking.

"Have you seen anyone with suitcases?"

"No, sorry—"

"No problem! You folks have a nice day!" he hollers, picking up speed again as I clutch the bar above for dear life.

We hear the warning honk of the ferry in the distance before we're even around the final corner.

"Shit," Alph hisses.

My heart sinks like a stone. "No. Oh, no."

Gravel sprays under the tires as Alph takes the corner at top speed, but somehow we stay upright. Then it's on to the final stretch, and into the parking lot.

He doesn't even bother parking properly, steering toward the turning area at the top of the wharf. "Go!"

I leap out of the moving golf cart. I feel like a cartoon,

legs whirling underneath me to keep pace with my body. Only willpower and desperation keeps me upright.

We're too late.

The ferry is chugging off into the distance, a little too far away to holler at it… but close enough that I can see a flash of bright yellow in the luggage area.

"No!"

The golf cart screeches to a halt and Alph's footsteps pound down the metal ramp after me.

I'm burning up with helpless fury. Gravity has seized hold of me, and I can't stop moving—even at the bottom of the ramp. With my eyes fixed on the ferry, I'm veering off to the side, heading right for the edge of the water.

I skid across the slick boards, arms whirling as I try to stay upright.

Alph grabs me by the back of my jacket. He grabs me around the waist by the other hand, hauling me back into him.

"Fuck," I gasp, my thighs shaking as I stare down at the murky blue water. That was way too close for comfort. I *definitely* don't have time to figure out a whole new outfit before the showcase.

If I even make it.

The ferry crossing is too quick. Even if we ran to the dock where the small boats moor, we couldn't beat them to the harbour in Alph's boat. They're already most of the way there.

Alph lets go of me and sprints to the bar. My lungs burn. I double over and press my hands on my thighs, catching my breath. I'm surprised at how quickly I recover, though.

All that hauling fabric on and off the island has really done me wonders.

I push the door open, tailing Alph to the bar.

"—Ronan's assistant," Kieran is animatedly waving his hands at Alph. "Not even an hour ago. He didn't want to interrupt you two, so I told him where you live."

"Fuck." Kieran turns his confused stare to me. "I don't *have* an assistant. But I do have enemies."

Kieran freezes, staring between me and Alph. "Oh, *bollocking* fuck."

Alph leans over to look out the window at the ferry—it's made it past the open water in the middle, where the float-planes land. That means it's just about in the harbour.

And then Derek and his cronies are home free.

Alph braces one forearm against the top of the bar and flings himself across. I gasp, Kieran leaps out of the way, and Alph grabs a radio hanging on the back wall.

"Sunbeam, this is Sunrise Harbour. Come in," he barks into it.

I hold my breath as the line crackles.

"This is the Sunbeam, over."

It's his boss, Berty.

"Instruction," Alph says, staring out the window at the ferry. "Return to Sunrise Harbour. I repeat, instruction: return to Sunrise Harbour."

Please, please, please... I can't breathe. I cross my fingers for dear life, leaning on the bar and waiting as the radio crackles.

"I will return to Sunrise Harbour."

Kieran whoops and pumps his fist. I groan with relief, sagging against the counter. There's only a few people in the restaurant at this hour, but they're all cheering, too.

Then the radio crackles again and Alph raises his hand, shushing everyone.

"Pan pan." I squint at it, trying to figure out what I just

heard, but I don't dare ask. Alph's jaw is suddenly, and Kieran is dead silent. "MV Sunbeam has lost three persons overboard. I repeat: three persons overboard."

I clap a hand over my mouth. "It's them," I hiss. "It has to be!"

The Coast Guard is on the line all of a sudden. I can barely follow the back-and-forth, but Alph mutters explanations. "They're refusing the ferry's assistance. Berty's coming back here."

I scramble to the window, only half-listening to Alph's explanations as I watch the ferry looming closer. Above all else, there's only one thing I care about.

Are my suitcases still on board?

Alph grunts and slaps the radio down. "They're out of the water. Sounds like they swam to the dock."

But the ferry is close, so I yank the door open—and then I stumble to a halt.

A small crowd has already formed by the ferry slip. Some clutch coffees as they murmur furiously with each other, pointing at the incoming boat.

"What's going on?" someone asks Alph. "Why's it coming all the way back?"

Instantly, he's cool and calm. "There's stolen goods aboard that ferry, and the owner would like them back."

"Do you mean those three kids?" gasps one of the restaurant patrons.

"And the suitcases? I saw them!" says someone who just came down the ramp from the coffee shop.

"I gave them directions!"

One of the white-haired ladies from the committee snorts and folds her arms. "I gave them a ride!" She looks furious. "They were *stealing* from you?" I nod jerkily. "Well, I'm going to kick those suitcases right up their—"

"They jumped off the ferry," Kieran calls out, beaming as he joins us. "Crawled out onto the dock like drowned rats, rather than face the music. Bunch of cowards."

"You can't rescue someone who doesn't want to be rescued," Alph says softly, walking down the ferry slip as the ferry shuts off its engines and drifts up close. Berty tosses him a rope, and he swiftly loops it around the closest cleat.

But my eyes are fixed on the luggage area, where I can see two bright flashes of yellow.

A cheer rises among the onlookers.

Oh, my god.

My knees almost give way with relief as I wobble, grabbing the post at the corner of the dock to keep myself upright.

Berty stands at the step inside the ferry and offers me a hand. "Hop aboard, you two," he says. "Let's get this ferry on the move."

My gut wrenches as I look up at Alph.

He gazes down at me solemnly, a muscle twitching in his jaw. There's a pained look in his eyes, but he seems to expect it already.

My stuff might be here, but I can't pretend nothing happened.

This was very nearly the biggest disaster of my life. And we both know who's responsible for it.

Now that I'm not scared, I'm just pissed.

"You may as well stay here. They won't let you in until showtime," I tell Alph, my shoulders tight as I stare up at him.

I want him to fight. I want him to tell me that he *wants* to come with me, even if he can't.

Alph sighs, closes his eyes, and bows his head to kiss the top of my head. "Tell me if you need anything," he says.

Fuck.

I thought we were past this.

Fury knots in my chest and tightens every muscle in my body. And there's one thought I just can't shake. If the door between our apartments had been locked... none of this would have happened.

"A locked door," I murmur, even if he won't meet my eyes. "If not outside, then inside."

Alph flinches, but he doesn't say anything—he just takes the hit as I take Berty's hand and step down into the ferry.

My legs still shaking under me, I collapse in the seat next to the luggage rack, keeping my back to the dock.

The boat casts off, and Berty strides to the cockpit. "All right, folks. Let's get underway..." The engine kicks in.

As the cold salt air whips through my hair, it's all I can do not to stare over my shoulder at Alph. I clear my throat, nails digging into my knees. Finally, I manage to look up at the handful of fellow passengers on board.

"S-Sorry, guys. For the delay." I pat my suitcases, feeling guilty all of a sudden. "I really, *really* needed these today."

All the sympathetic murmurs and head shakes are too much to bear. Even Berty, renowned for talking people's ears off, doesn't say much on the intercom for the whole crossing.

I can't stop fidgeting with the locks on the suitcase zippers. I'm just grateful they're still closed and locked—and that my asshole ex-roomies didn't decide to throw them in the harbour.

Finally, I can't stop myself. I twist to look over my shoulder. The crowd has dispersed, but Alph is still standing there. He's still as a statue, one hand shielding his eyes.

My heart twinges, and it feels like I'm breaking into pieces. But even pressing my hand on my chest and rubbing doesn't help.

He did rescue me... from the situation he created...

I shake my head and gulp the cold air, turning back to face the harbour instead.

Alph trusts people too easily, and I can't let that rub off on me.

Of all people, *I* know better. But it's ironic, really. It wasn't even serial killers in the end. It was so much worse.

Alph's always trying to be so responsible in every other way. Why not this one little thing? After all these weeks we've both sacrificed, why take the slightest chance that anything could go wrong?

He helped me trust people again… but now that feels like a mistake. I don't even know if I can trust *him,* and that's the worst feeling I can possibly imagine.

CHAPTER
Twenty-Six
ALPH

This was all my fault.

After everything we've been through together, *I* was the one who nearly screwed Ronan over. So, so, *so* badly. And the worst part is exactly how it all went down.

He kept bugging me about locking the fucking doors. I have plenty of excuses, but none of them are good enough. The truth is plain and simple.

I let him down.

There's no worse feeling than letting someone down about anything, however minor. And this is the biggest possible way I could have let him down. That's what hurts the most: knowing that Ronan's right to be furious with me.

I fucked this one up, big-time.

The ferry is long out of sight, but I'm still standing here staring into space.

"Hey. Get in here," Kieran's voice pierces the fog in my brain. When I do, he orders me to sit my ass down, and then he presses a glass into my hand.

A beer?

I glance up at him and blink. "On the house?" Kieran half-smiles, and I wish I could laugh, but I'm too miserable.

"Thanks—" I sip, then squint at it. "Is this that… zero percent stuff?"

"I want you to move your golf cart later. It's blocking the ramp," Kieran tells me, and I manage a huff of breath that almost passes for a laugh.

"Fine. A beer's a beer, I guess." I didn't realize how dry my throat is, and to be honest, it's a relief to gulp it down faster than my usual stuff. "Oh, god. I really fucked this up."

"Mate," Kieran winces as he leans on the counter. "If anyone fucked this up, it was me. And the dozen other people here who helped them out," he gestures furiously toward the island. "We had no idea there was sabotage."

I should warned them. I should have thought about that myself.

"Whoa," Kieran snaps his fingers. "Stop giving yourself reasons to feel guilty. Take it from me: you go down that road, there's no end to it."

"So what do I do?" I look up at him.

Kieran hums thoughtfully, scrubbing down the bar with a rag. "You can't go lock that door now."

"True."

"And you can't go after him until the show opens."

"No, yeah." I hesitate, glancing over the harbour again. "But… I wanted to. And I should have tried. Even if I can't get what I want… I'm supposed to be honest about it."

"Mmm." Kieran folds his arms on the bar to watch me. "So what now?"

"I can't do anything." I grunt with frustration. "I just wait around until this evening. I mean… I was planning something else, but... oh, god." I fold my arms on the bar and bump my forehead against them.

It's too little, too late. I don't even know if he's going to want to come home to me later.

"Here's an idea."

When I look up, Kieran has turned the CCTV monitor toward me. There's three figures walking past the camera, and one of them turns to look over his shoulder.

"Derek," I hiss quietly. "That's him."

Then, Kieran picks up his cellphone and turns it to me, too. He swipes between two photos: a blurry photo of all three of them just inside the front gate, and another photo of them crowded around the yellow suitcases like they're trying to block them from sight.

"Idiots," I scoff.

Kieran grins. "Does this help give you something to do today?"

"Hell, yeah." That's one way I can make amends. And not just for Ronan's sake—because I want to, too. Those assholes took advantage of me, and nobody gets away with that anymore.

Then my phone buzzes, and for a moment, my hopes rise.

CARTER:

We're here. Are you coming?

Shit. He hasn't heard the news. Should I call the whole thing off?

Kieran is being nosy, leaning over to read my phone as he dries glasses. "Oh, aye. That's true. If I overheard you and the lads right the other day, you've got somewhere to be."

"You... you really think it'll fix things?" I look up, biting my lip.

I made this plan weeks ago, when I couldn't have predicted how badly today would go wrong. It's a risky move. But if I'm already in the doghouse, how much worse could things get?

Kieran shrugs. "Maybe it will, maybe it won't." He sets down the glass and looks at me. "But there's a chance it will."

A chance. I'd do anything for another chance.

"Prince Charming would take the chance."

"Yeah," I breathe out, making up my mind. I have to make up for everything that's happened today—however I can. I set down my glass and push back the stool. "Thanks, Kieran. Wish me luck!"

I'll need it.

CHAPTER
Twenty-Seven

RONAN

I have no idea how my roommates made it.

They *look* like they got dunked in the harbour. They're clearly dressed in borrowed clothes, hair flattened and shoes squelching… but they're there.

Whatever.

There's no time to think, or cuss them out, or do anything. Not if I'm going to do the best I possibly can at this showcase. Right now, that's what matters.

Professor Meyer has been warning us for weeks how frantic this is going to be. But it really *is* just go go go, with barely time to breathe. Dressing models, making sure the makeup is right, styling, last-minute alterations…

Then I turn to start work on my final touch—the one thing that will tie all my looks together—and I freeze.

"Shit. Shit, shit, shit."

I didn't bring the roll of marine chain. I was planning to cut, drape, and sew it onto each outfit in a slightly different way… and it's not here.

Think...! I cast my mind to the small hours. *Shit. I put it in a different bag.*

It was sitting next to the suitcase, but it obviously wasn't there, or I would have seen it.

Did they bring it? Did I forget it on the ferry, then? Or did they fling it into the corner of the living room when they trashed my sewing studio?

I hiss as I turn on the spot, glaring toward Derek's work station.

"Something wrong?" Derek asks smugly. He's barely had any alterations to make at all, in fact. He's just been sitting here on his phone for the last two hours.

Like someone else did all the work.

"No," I snap at him and turn my back.

The last thing I can do is *ask*. They'll lie to my face and laugh about it. But if I don't have it in under an hour... I'm fucked.

There's nothing else strong enough that ties together the six looks. I was counting on this. I know what I have to swallow my pride and do, so I pull out my phone and tap Alph's name.

RONAN:

I need something.

ALPH:

Anything.

His response is instant, but my chest is too tight to breathe as I furiously tap at my phone.

RONAN:

There's a roll of chain. It was in the living room in a bag.

I lean on my workstation and breathe out shakily, pressing my phone to my forehead.

"Listen up," Professor Meyer calls out from the front of the room. She points to a piece of paper on the wall. "The final running order."

We all put down what we're doing to rush over, leaning in to squint at the page. Like the rest of my classmates, I scan for my name—and I keep on scanning.

Derek's standing right at my elbow. "Last," he mutters to me, and my eyes jump to the bottom to confirm what he's saying. "So everyone else can leave."

I won't let him make me lose my cool again today. I just straighten up, nose crinkling as I step away from him. "So you can take a shower before you watch me beat you."

Then I blush, glancing sideways at Professor Meyer. I don't want to sound cocky, after all.

I could swear she's smiling. She walks down the middle

of the aisle, hands folded in front of her as she looks over our models.

"Be ready in time," she finally says, her glance lingering on my models. She turns to look at me. "Whatever it takes."

As we rush back to our workstations, Gabby whispers, "Your chain! Where is it?" I shrug, and she winces. "I've got some extra stuff…"

I shake my head. "It's okay. Thanks. Alph's on his way."

Gabby bites her lip. I've only told her a little bit of what happened, in whispers. "Yeah? You sure?"

"Alph won't leave me stranded."

She nods and strides off to keep on working, and I sink onto my chair and run my hands through my hair.

I have to believe that.

I just have to.

Just as I'm starting to sweat, I hear a familiar grunt.

"Alph."

I spin on my heel, and relief hits me hard. Despite everything, the sight of him sweating and hauling a box over to my workstation…

It makes my heart soar.

The minute he walks in, I feel safe. More than that. I feel like I can fly again.

I don't even care that Alph's dressed in torn old jeans and a paint-stained T-shirt, like he's been digging around the backyard shed.

I'm pretty sure he actually has. There's bolt cutters that look like they're from his own tool kit, and underneath… chains, in all different sizes.

"I stopped by the repair shed—"

I don't care. I grab him by both cheeks and haul him down to kiss him on the mouth.

Alph goes rigid with surprise, but only for half a second. Then he melts and wraps his arms around my waist, kissing me back until I'm out of breath and dizzy.

"Now, how can I help?"

I don't even bat an eye. "Cut it for me," I tell him, beckoning one of my models over. "I'll tell you where."

Alph grabs the bolt cutters from the top of the box, and I peer down into it. The chains are different sizes and colours. There's a bunch that looks similar to what I'd picked out… but there's other stuff that looks used.

That's what I go for first. I grab a reel and set to work.

Time vanishes as I call over each model, one at a time. I work my way around them, standing back to judge what I should use and where. I drape and re-drape, stitch furiously, and point out links for Alph to cut.

And then… as quickly as the rush starts, it's over.

"Thirty minutes to runway," comes the announcement over the intercom. "Quiet backstage, please. The doors are opening. Your models should be ready."

Just in the nick of time.

"Are we done?" Alph asks me.

I breathe out a sigh, dropping the last length of chain back into the crate as I sink onto the stool in front of my workbench. "We're done."

"I'd better get back out there, then," Alph says, and then he grins ruefully as he looks down at himself. "If they'll even let me sit out there."

I can't help giggling. It's ironic that I don't have anything to spare…

Except, I do.

"The shirt," I gasp, and Alph perks up as I laugh.

It was the last thing in the suitcase last night. I wanted to bring it with me today to remind me how far I've come.

I didn't plan on anyone wearing it.

"Here," I tell him, handing the damn thing over to Alph. That familiar feeling of embarrassment is back—tenfold worse, knowing he's going to be sitting there in the audience wearing it.

But when I watch him put it on, something changes.

It's way too big for me, which means it fits Alph. The red lace picks something up in his hair, and with the ripped jeans and T-shirt…

It's like he planned this look on purpose.

"Does it look all right?" Alph asks.

"Yes, but—stop," I laugh under my breath, slapping his hands away before he can button it up all the way. I pop most of them open again. "Leave the T-shirt showing."

He squints in confusion and gives up, shrugging. "I trust you."

My throat suddenly feels tight. I carefully take his hands in mine. His palms are covered in grease from the chains and bolt cutters, but I turn them palm-up, kissing them one at a time.

"And I trust you."

Alph's breath rushes out. He curls his hands into fists, and a little smile appears on his face.

"I'll see you on the other side," I tell him as a stage hand approaches, no doubt prepared to usher Alph away as we assemble backstage. "Get going."

"I'll be here," Alph promises, low and fierce. "No matter what."

Then he kisses me, and I'm done.

All I can do is wait.

Sometimes you end up stranded on Maple Island because you need to be saved. And sometimes you have to trust that you've done everything you can to save yourself.

It's time to find out which way the tide is rushing.

CHAPTER
Twenty-Eight

RONAN

I HAVE NO IDEA WHAT TO EXPECT.

Each classmate heads out to take a bow after their models. Sometimes, the applause is quiet and polite—for my three roommates—and other times, enthusiastic.

Then, they breathlessly stumble backstage with bouquets of flowers, wearing a grin or a weary grimace… and the lights go dark again.

It's finally my turn.

After all these months, it all comes down to a few minutes that might as well be a few seconds.

Walk… and walk… and walk…

It's over.

I clasp my hands tightly in front of my chest, waiting. I can barely breathe. I don't know what people thought. Maybe they *did* save me for last so everyone's friends and family can leave—

Then I hear Professor Meyer.

"Ronan Ashfield!"

It's my cue. My legs are shaking, but my classmates grin and shove me to the gap in the black curtains.

I stumble through, and as I emerge from the dim light backstage into the light, the wave of applause almost knocks me off my feet.

What?

I blink and stumble to a halt, staring breathlessly around. My models are clapping with raised hands, beaming at me.

There's Alph, standing at the edge of the stage and grinning up at me, holding a bouquet of roses. Behind him, I see my parents—and both of my brothers—standing up to applaud as they watch me with so much pride.

Even Professor Meyer is smiling.

I stumble forward to accept the bouquet of roses in one hand. With the other, I blow Alph a kiss, leaning down to make sure he can hear me. "Alph. I couldn't have done it without you."

Alph catches the kiss and presses it against his lips, smiling right back up at me. "You could have," he tells me over the noise. "But you don't have to."

Tears spring to my eyes. I raise the bouquet and bury my face in it, and the applause fades into chuckles and murmurs.

Professor Meyer is talking about me and the collection. And thank god, because I couldn't think of anything smart to say right now. All her words sound much better.

Groundbreaking, raw talent to keep an eye on.

That's the only phrase that sticks in my brain, and I replay it over and over. I catch Alph's eye as he sits down again, and he just winks at me.

There's another round of applause, and I bow again, and then Professor Meyer calls out the rest of my classmates, and all of the models.

After the bows, one of us—definitely me—loses their cool first, and the rest follow. We're jumping and whooping and hollering as we hug each other, celebrating the fact that we survived.

Well, almost all of us. Obviously, there are three people sullenly huddled at the back of the group, but not even they can drag down our mood.

We did it!

And I'm not counting my chickens before they hatch... but I think *I* did it.

There's just one thing left to do.

With a few final hugs, we separate ourselves to wait by our workstations, each of us surrounded by our own cluster of models. Our friends and family aren't here yet.

Professor Meyer is talking with the representatives. Any minute now, we're going to find out how we did—and what we'll be doing next semester. The anticipation is killing me.

When she appears, I clap a hand over my mouth. It's all I can do not to jump out of my skin as she strides toward us all, bright red heels clicking against the floors.

She's carrying a stack of folders in her arms, making a beeline this way. Heading for...

Please be me, please be me!

"Derek."

What? My mouth falls open.

At least I'm not the only one. The rest of my classmates gasp, trading glances with each other and looking at me.

Even Derek stares at Professor Meyer for a moment, open-mouthed, as she slaps a thick folder against his chest.

Then he starts to smirk again, shooting a triumphant look at me.

I feel sick.

"Open it."

He puts it down and flips it open, crossing one ankle casually over the other like he's the king of the castle… and then he freezes.

So do I. Even if it's upside-down and grainy, like a photocopy of a photocopy… I recognize that drawing.

It's mine.

Professor Meyer flips the pages in front of his eyes, showing him everything inside. I recognize a lot of it. My sketches from last year, brainstorming lists that I thought were long gone, you name it.

Then, abruptly, crude drawings—side-by-side with the very same ones I've seen him show us in class, like bad copies. Or bad originals.

Derek is white as a ghost. "What…" he trails off, and then he whips his head around to hiss at me. "You? You little—"

Professor Meyer clears her throat, and the words die on his lips.

"You didn't think I'd know everyone in the province who has the skill—the creative vision—needed to create a collection like this?" She slams the folder closed again. "That nobody would talk to me before applying for a job at a new brand? When the studio is in my own city? Right under my nose?"

Derek just stutters wordlessly.

I glance over at Breanna and Shane, and then I grin. Their models are preventing them from sneaking away by linking arms, forming human walls.

"Breanna," Professor Meyer says. "Shane." She walks past

their work benches and slams an equally thick folder on each.

I can't bring myself to feel bad.

I'd bet my bottom dollar they wanted me to quit school so they could just straight-up rip off my ideas, without even covering their tracks.

Unlike them, I love what I do—and I actually *do* what I say I'm doing.

Thank god they burned that bridge with me, and set me free.

"You don't think I'd recognise the same art style in all your portfolios?" Professor Meyer tells the three of them. "Or the source of all your best ideas?"

Then she walks toward me.

I gulp hard, glancing at the thin folder pressed between two fingers. She slides it across the workstation, taps it with one bright red nail, and waits.

I didn't help them on purpose, I swear. I bite back my defense, waiting for her to say something.

"Open it."

I do, and then I blink.

It's… a job description? No, it's a work experience offer, with a blank signature line for me to sign. And right at the top, in neat bolded text, is the answer I'm looking for.

XX Gracieux.

I gasp. "No."

"That wasn't the answer I was expecting," she tells me, and she's actually smiling.

"I mean—yes! God, yes!" My classmates cover their chuckles with coughs. "Thank you, Professor. I just—I— thank you."

Professor nods slightly. "You deserve it, Ronan."

Then she turns to stare at the others. "Those three groups of models—thank you for your time. You can all go home. Breanna, Shane, Derek—be in my office in twenty minutes."

Derek's voice croaks. "Yes, ma'am," he says. "Of course. To discuss, uh… the options for our future here?"

The guy's got brass balls. I stare at him in disbelief, and my classmates cover their snorts and grumbles.

Professor Meyer actually laughs. "No. The cops wanted somewhere they wouldn't be disturbed. Now, go."

Oh my god. Alph reported them! With all the chaos, there wasn't a minute to even think about it today. But he took care of it for me.

He took care of me.

As our disgraced fellow students leave, Professor Meyer twitches a finger at a stage hand waiting by the curtain. "Let the families in now. Thank you."

Friends and families stream in as she starts walking around the room, laying a folder on each workstation. She stops to talk to each of us about it, and I can't help noticing that everyone actually looks happy about their placement.

I still can't believe that I got the most coveted job of all.

"Ronan!" Alph gasps, rushing up to me. My parents and brothers are following, but they're slowed down by staring wide-eyed at all the chaos backstage. "Did you get it?"

"I got it!" I fling my arms around his shoulders, and he picks me up and spins me around as he whoops.

I laugh, squirming in protest.

"If I can interrupt you," Professor Meyer says drily, and Alph clears his throat.

"Yes, ma'am," he says and plops me back on my feet as my

parents and brothers join him. They're staring at everything backstage, but especially my models.

I pull my gaze off them and look back at my teacher.

"Ronan," she says, nodding. "I was worried about you at the end of last year. But you came back a new person. Something changed."

"Yeah." I clear my throat. "Right before classes started, I realized you were right. It's like when you're walking down the sidewalk and you collide with people." She tilts her head, and I shrug. "I was looking where I was trying *not* to go. I just eventually got lucky enough to run right into what I actually needed."

Professor Meyer nods at last, looking over at Alph. "I'd tell you what a gem you've found, but I think you already know."

"Yes, ma'am."

"He's got some more tumbling to do before he graduates… but you keep looking after him, all right?"

"He is," Alph agrees with a good-natured smile, glancing nervously at me over the bouquet he's still clutching. "I sure plan to."

"Congratulations," she tells me, and then she strides off before I can say another word.

The models are filtering out now, and our obligations are wrapping up. I want to say something to Alph, but my family's rushing close. They all hug me. Mom, Dad, both my brothers.

"You know, I think… I get it now," Dad says, pulling back to scratch his head as he watches the retreating models like he's searching for data he can use. Then he shakes his head and looks at me. "More than before, anyway."

My mom ruffles my hair, pushing the blond strands back

into place. "We can see that you're happy now," she says quietly. "This isn't making you miserable anymore."

Was it really? I swallow hard, casting my mind back to the summer, and my stomach twists. I think she's right. I was so consumed by my fear of what I didn't want... that I'd lost sight of what I *do* want.

"I'm sorry," Dad tells me. He clasps my shoulders until I look at him. "For what we said—about not supporting you for the last semester. We thought..." he clears his throat and lets go of one shoulder to wipe his eyes. I put my hand on Dad's, silently shaking my head as my eyes water. "We thought we were offering you a way out."

I pull him in and hug him tightly, and then I wipe my eyes. "In a way... you did."

One man's chains are another man's freedom. That's why I chose chains to link together the looks in my mini-collection—and not just any chains, but marine chains.

My dad pulls back and clears his throat while my brothers slap me on the back and grin.

"Hey! Sweet shirt," Garrett says, nodding at the shirt Alph's wearing.

Alph grins. "Thanks. I got it from the best new designer in town."

"Oh—oh yeah. Um. Mom, Dad, Garrett, Reid... this is Alph."

All of them are laughing. Alph takes my hand and squeezes it. "We sat together for the show," he reminds me gently. "We've met now."

Oh. Right.

"Let's get out of here to the afterparty!" yells one of my classmates.

"We'll leave you to celebrate," Mom tells me, kissing my cheek. "I'm proud of you, Ronan."

"And it's very nice to meet your boyfriend," Dad adds, shaking hands with Alph.

Alph shifts the bouquet in the crook of his arm and glances at me ruefully, the question in his eyes.

I smile. I can't tear my gaze away from his. "Yeah," I answer. "It is."

After our families leave—and after the cleanup—Alph finally takes my suitcases, one in each hand.

"I just have one—"

"I gotta ask—"

I laugh. "You go first," I tell him.

He beams at me and wraps an arm around my shoulders. "Even if I'm kind of an idiot sometimes... I've been so pleased, so proud, to call you my betrothed boyfriend these past few months."

My cheeks flush as my breathing quickens.

"I think you know what I want. At least, I hope so, by now." Alph laughs, and I realize his hand is actually trembling slightly on my back. "Ronan... will you be my boyfriend?"

"Oh, Alph." I cup his cheek in my hand. "I already am. And you know what? I think I have been all along."

Alph beams as wide as the sun, and then he kisses me.

It feels like an eternity before we pull apart to the sound of wolf-whistling and cheers from my classmates.

Then, Gabby claps her hands once. "And *now* we party!"

"Your turn," Alph says at last, and I blink at him. "You had a question."

"Oh, right." I giggle, bouncing at his side as he rolls along the suitcases. "How'd you find them?"

Alph raises his eyebrow. "It's obvious. I looked for the accountants."

I laugh, and then I stand on tiptoe to kiss Alph, and—at long last—I feel it.

All is well.

CHAPTER
Twenty~Nine

ALPH

I'M STILL PRETTY SURE I SHOULDN'T BE ALLOWED IN Nanaimo's sleekest lounge dressed like this… but thanks to Professor Meyer, we're in the VIP area for the afterparty.

After hearing about all of Ronan's classmates for so long, I'm happy to meet them. Better still, I get to hear him talking in his own language to people who get it—even if I don't understand a word of what they're saying.

He really is going places.

And he deserves it.

Derek, Breanna, and Shane, on the other hand? I don't think anyone's going to miss them. And what with Ronan getting the work placement of his dreams, I think his last semester will be the best of all.

I want to let Ronan bask in the glow for as long as possible, but I know all too well when the ferry leaves for the last trip of the day to Sunrise Island.

"Hey," Ronan greets me, looping his arm around mine and giggling as he sips his glass of champagne. "What's the worried face?"

I clear my throat sheepishly as he grins up at me. There's no point in pretending he hasn't busted me.

"Thinking about the last ferry timing. I mean, I could ask someone to help us out. It's just…"

They've already done a huge favour for me today… but I want that to keep that a surprise for now.

Ronan shakes his head before I can even think up an excuse. "No," he tells me simply and stretches up to kiss my cheek. "I want to go. I've done everything I needed to do. I'm ready."

I smile at him. "Yeah?" I ask, biting off my apology about living on an island before it can even start. "You're not feeling like such a night owl these days?"

Ronan giggles. "I'm going to need a lot more sleep, if I'm going to go places. Besides, my boyfriend works shifts. I want to share some of those early mornings with him."

All I can do is grin stupidly at him until he laughs and pecks my lips, and then I follow along in his wake, hugging and shaking hands until we've said goodbye to the whole room.

"Eep!" Ronan finally squeaks when he realizes he's starting the second round of goodbyes, and we're on a time crunch. "Are we good?"

"We're good," I promise, taking him by the hand and squeezing it firmly. "I promise."

Right on time, we're walking toward the harbour, our fingers laced tightly together. Each of us is rolling along one of the suitcases in the other hand.

It's a clear, crisp night, but Ronan seems perfectly warm. He's still practically bouncing at my side, high on life.

Meanwhile, I just feel… calm.

Deep, calm, and still, like the harbour waters. The storm has settled, and the whitecaps are long gone.

Everything's going to be okay.

Ronan perches on the wooden bench in the ferry waiting room, peering out over the water. He sighs with contentment, finally settling down as he looks at me.

"Happy?" I smile at him.

Ronan nods. "I've got everything I need. My skipper right here, and his ferry. Ready for a starlight tour, all the way home."

I smile sheepishly at him and clear my throat. "Actually, that reminds me… I've been waiting to tell you something."

"Oh?" Ronan peers up at me.

I clear my throat. "Yesterday morning, Berty and I signed off the paperwork on something I've been wanting to do for a while."

Ronan perks up. "Ooooh. An electric ferry?"

"No," I laugh, squeezing his hand. I'm impressed at his memory. "Well… not yet. He's agreed to let me run a tour. Once a week in the winter, to iron out the wrinkles. If it goes well, more often in the summer. If it goes really well… yes, an electric ferry."

Ronan stares at me, clutching my hand in both of his. "You're really doing it?" he whispers. "You're going for it?"

I clear my throat and nod. "You're looking at the new, official owner of Sunrise Island Tours."

"Oh my god!" Ronan squeaks. He launches himself at me, flinging his arms around my shoulders. I catch him and laugh, waiting patiently for his face to turn to mine—and then I kiss him.

Our lips slide together gently, but the passion in our kiss is a barely-restrained fire.

I'm only keeping it in check because the ferry is about to dock. I want to save all that fire for when we get home, and I can show Ronan what he means to me.

"I'm so proud of you," Ronan breathes out when he finally scrambles off my lap so we can stand up.

"Me, too," I admit with a grin. "Feels good to go for what you want."

Something pinches my ass, and I gasp with surprise as Ronan giggles mischievously.

"It sure does, hot stuff."

* * *

After a quiet late-night ferry crossing, I'm a little bit overwhelmed by the noise and laughter spilling from Sunrise Island's bar. Part of me wants to head straight up the ramp.

But I think there's one more thing Ronan needs to know before I bring him home for good.

"Let's stick our heads in for a minute," I tell him. He pouts up at me, and I laugh. "Don't worry. I really do mean a minute. I know how much sleep you got last night."

"Okay," Ronan murmurs.

I park the suitcases outside the bar's door and push it open. "After you."

The moment Ronan walks in, he's greeted with cheers from all our friends and neighbours. He stumbles to a halt and stares around at everyone, a blush creeping up his cheeks.

"How'd it go?" Kieran calls across the bar.

"Did you get that job you wanted?" That's the new barista, Harley.

Marianne's sitting in the corner with a glass of sherry. "Did you jam those suitcases right up their jacked-up little—"

Laughter drowns out her next suggestion.

I slide my arm around Ronan's shoulders, encouraging him into the middle of the room. "Best in his class," I brag, since he's still too tongue-tied. "And… tell them, sweetie."

Ronan smiles dizzily around at everyone. "I—I got the work placement. And they got kicked out of the school."

The room erupts into cheers and whistles again as people raise their glasses to him. They gradually return to their conversations, and Ronan turns to whisper in my ear.

"What was that all about? Did you tell them?"

I blink at him. "Tell them what?"

"About today?" Ronan nods like it's obvious, and I chuckle and shake my head. "No, sweetie. *You* did."

"Me? But I… I can't have." He scrunches up his nose. "I've been in my own head. You know that better than anyone. I haven't been… *here*."

I smile at him. "Yeah, you have. You know when you run into the coffee shop? You're always nice to the staff. At the store, you ask how everyone's day is going. You know the names of all Marianne's chickens. On the ferry, you help people with their shopping bags."

Ronan looks at me and squints. "I… I guess so? But… are you spying on me?"

"I don't need to. Island life," I grin. "Everything gets back to everyone. And those things you do are invisible to you, because they're who you are. But they show everyone around you who you are, too."

"Oh," Ronan murmurs softly, and the wrinkles in his forehead smooth out. "I just… didn't think they noticed."

I smile as I lean in to press a kiss on his forehead. "People can't help but notice you, sweetheart. I'm just glad you're finally letting them."

Ronan blinks back tears as he wraps his arms around my waist, a sigh rushing from him. Then he pulls back and clears his throat. "What's the next event on the calendar here? Downhill skiing in dishwashers?"

I crack up, turning us around to point at the posters in the doorway. "The winter festival, next week."

"Can we go?" Ronan takes my hand, smiling shyly at me. "Now that people seem to know me… I'd like to get to know them, too." He clears his throat. "After all… this is home."

I'm flooded with warmth and excitement all of a sudden, grinning right back at him. "Yeah. Of course. I'd love that."

Kieran coughs loudly, grabbing my attention. "Berty!" he claps our boss on the shoulder, interrupting him before he can make a beeline for me. "I've got a… stock question." Then, he shoots me a wink.

That's our cue to go.

As Ronan and I slip out into the night, I grab both suitcases and carry them up the ramp to the golf cart. I shove them into the back, and then I stand back. "So… I'm going to tell you what I want now."

"Please," Ronan whispers.

I step forward to scoop him right off the ground, safely into my arms. "I want to be home," I tell Ronan, kissing him right on the lips.

"Yes, please!"

"And… I want to take you."

"Oh, yes, please. Take me home—" Ronan breaks off, and then he giggles helplessly as he realizes exactly what I said. "Alph!"

"Mmhmm?" I grin wickedly. I lift him into the seat of the golf cart before striding around to the driver's side.

"You're getting good at this."

"I'm a fast learner," I promise with a wink, starting up the engine. "You'll see."

CHAPTER

Thirty

RONAN

Alph tugs me to a halt before I can head up the porch stairs. "Hey, Ronan? Let's head in through the back entrance."

I stand back to let him wrestle the suitcases down the cobblestone path around the side of the house. I'm perfectly happy to save my big, strong hunk any more staircases with those damn things.

"The back entrance?" I tease, trotting after him. "You don't need to ask me twice."

His eyes twinkle as he glances up at me. "I will anyway. I want to try everything with you. Twice, just to make sure."

The excitement is almost too much. I bite my lip, struggling to keep myself from jumping his bones right here and now. Just a few more steps and we'll be inside…

But first, apparently, there's a locked door.

We trade grins as Alph digs out his keys and unlocks the door, then pushes it open. He hefts the suitcases inside, and then he follows suit and turns on the lights.

"Come on in."

I step inside… and, for what feels like the hundredth time today, I stop in my tracks.

"What the…"

The dining room table is gone. The sofa and chairs have been moved to this spot, forming a little sitting area. To the left is a desk sitting by itself, tucked in next to the kitchen.

"That one's mine," Alph says when he notices me looking. Then he grins, like he's waiting for me to come to the inevitable conclusion.

I pivot to stare at the living room… which isn't a living room anymore. My whiteboards are all hanging up in a row on one wall. My mannequins—once shoved behind the sitting chairs upstairs—stand neatly in gaps between shelving units, which are all filled up with clear plastic bins.

My stuff—all of it, including the mess left behind by my ex-roommates—is in those bins. And they're all neatly labelled in Alph's handwriting.

In the middle of the room, there are two more desks, all set up for me to work from. And I swear I see on one of them…

"Is that my sewing machine?" I sprint over to it, my jaw dropping as I lean over to inspect it. "Holy shit. But it was…?"

"It wasn't the picture of health," Alph smiles at me. "But Marianne felt bad. She wanted to make up for it. And we're going to be baking her a *lot* of pies in return."

"So many pies."

I can't see the rest of it. My eyes are too blurry now, as tears trickle down my cheeks and I turn back to Alph.

"Is this really…?"

"Yes, Ronan," Alph murmurs. He steps closer and gently squeezes both my hands. "If you want it, it's yours."

I yank my hands out of his so I can wipe my eyes with both hands, and grab his great big silly face, and kiss him until the very air gives out from my lungs.

Alph moans sharply, his hands going to my waist as I finally pull away dizzily. "I take it that's a yes."

"*Fuck*, yes," I whisper. I'm still in shock. "Did you do all this today?"

"I had help. We were planning it for a while. That's why I left the door… um. You know." Alph clears his throat.

"Ohhhh," I groan with the realization. "Fuck. Really?"

"Yeah." Alph chuckles as he wraps me up in a hug. "I'm glad it went over well. Gotta admit, I've never spent so much time being so terrified while I build so much flatpack furniture."

I giggle softly, curling my hands into fists in his shirt. When I finally pull away to look at him, I clear my throat and dab my eyes again. "Alph. Fuck. I'm so sorry I freaked out at you."

"No," he says quickly as he strokes his fingertips through my hair, cupping my cheeks in his broad palms. "No, I'm sorry, Ronan. I should have been more responsible. I'll do whatever I need to do so that you feel safe in your home. In *our* home… and in your new studio."

I swallow the lump in my throat and breathe out a shaky sigh. "And I need to learn to have a little more trust in people."

Alph dabs my cheeks dry. "You want to see the upstairs now?"

"Please," I whisper. "Take me there."

Alph grins—and he scoops me right off my feet to sling me over his shoulder. "Aye aye."

I squeak in shock as the ground drops from under me. I

grab onto the back of Alph's shirt, but I can't even fight back. I'm laughing too hard… and, I have to admit, I'm more than a little turned on.

Alph doesn't even bother with the light switches. He just turns the corner to head straight down the hallway until we get to the master bedroom. Then he flicks the light on and tosses me onto the mattress.

"Whoa!" I laugh as I bounce against the bed, grinning up at him. "I love it when you put those muscles to good use."

He grins at me and crawls onto the bed, crouching over me. "Oh, yeah? Well, I love it when you put that imagination to good use."

"Mmm?" I beam at him. "You want me to tell you some of the things I've been imagining lately?"

Alph's hands rise to my shirt. He pops one button at a time open, keeping his eyes locked with mine and never looking away. "Tell me," he murmurs, his voice low and rough.

I bite my lip and squirm, my toes curling with excitement. When I try to unbutton his shirt, though, he knocks my hand away.

"You've dressed enough people today," he tells me. "I'm going to do the undressing for both of us. Now, spill."

Oh, fuck. I love that bossy voice.

"I, um…" I blush, wriggling as he slips one hand into my open shirt to run across my chest.

"Mmhmm?" Alph tweaks one nipple, then runs his thumb around it as he watches my reactions.

"Ah!" I can't help myself. "I—*fuck!*"

"You fuck?" Alph whispers. "Or *I* fuck *you?*

He rips the next few buttons open all at once and dips his head, wrapping his lips around my nipple instead. The tip of his tongue runs across the nub in slow, maddening circles, and I'm almost levitating off the bed. "

"Both. All of it. Always. Yes. That…!" I whimper.

"Tell me more," Alph growls against my chest. He flicks his tongue across my nipple, hard. Then, he starts kissing his way to the other side.

"Nnnnh!" I whimper, squirming against the sheets. "Nnf… mmm…" I swallow hard, gasping for breath. "I—I—I can't. I can't think. I can't talk. Not when you're—oh, fuck…!"

Alph chuckles deeply. "So far, so good." He tears the last button of my shirt open, hauling it off me to throw it aside. Then, he does the same for himself—only he takes a little more care with my creation.

"Fuck," I groan as he runs his palms down my bare torso, panting as I arch up into his touch. "Fuck, please…"

Alph grins, popping the button on my pants open with one hand. He slides his other palm over the hard line in my trousers. "Please what?"

"Naked. Now. Please."

I'm losing the ability to form sentences. All I can do is beg. I'm trying to cling to the fragmented fantasies he's asking me to call up—but reality is *so* much better.

Alph grins and gets to work, stripping both of us naked in what feels like seconds. But he never stops taking the chance to touch me: he runs his palms along my torso, dips his tongue to the hollow of my hips, grazes his teeth across my thighs…

"Fuck!"

I nearly leap clear off the bed when his lips brush the tip of my cock.

He chuckles and pushes me back down, easily holding me

there with one muscled forearm across my chest. Then he repeats himself, kissing gently across the tip and down the shaft.

"Oh… oh…!" I whimper, my thighs twitching. "Alph, I…" Then I choke and gasp at the same time. "Fuck!"

He's wrapping his lips around the head of my cock, and he's taking me into his mouth—slowly but surely. The wet heat of his mouth races through me in sharp, electric waves.

He starts bobbing his head, and I'm lost in heaven. My whole body is crackling to life like never before. I grab his shoulders and knead them hard, grit my teeth, push up into his mouth…

"Alph," I whimper at last, spreading my thighs wide open. "The lube. Please."

He grunts around my cock, toying his tongue against the head until my eyes roll back in my head and I shiver.

Don't cum… don't cum…!

Just in time, Alph pulls his head away from me with a wet pop and chuckles deeply. "Not bad for a first try?"

"Mmmmngh."

My senseless groan makes him laugh. He shifts on the bed, reaching over to grab the lube from my bedside table, and then he kneels between my legs and cracks the lube open. "Shall I?"

My whole body is still shivering pleasantly. The wet heat on my shaft is cooling in the bedroom air, giving me a whole new set of wonderful sensations to fight back. "Mmnh."

"Okay," Alph laughs, gently pressing a kiss against my inner thigh. "I've got you, sweetheart."

I spread my thighs for him and grin, closing my eyes as I tremble with anticipation. His cool, wet fingertips swipe between my legs, and then one finger rubs in slow, gentle circles—around my hole, and finally in.

The initial sharp sting softens into something more gentle and fizzy. I moan softly and relax on the bed, breathing out as Alph slides one finger into me. Little by little, he works me open, adding another finger… and a lot more lube.

When I feel those first sparks lighting up inside me, I gasp. "Yes," I groan. "Right there."

Alph strokes against the sensitive spot inside me again, and within seconds, he's figuring it out on his own. All he has to do is listen to what makes me moan or grunt or whimper, and do more of it.

I'm on fire with it now, burning up with my need. I don't think anyone could blame me for saying this… but I can't wait much longer.

"Please," I whimper, reaching down to touch Alph's wrist. "I want you. All of you."

His eyes soften. He pulls his fingers out of me so gently, and then he leans down to kiss my forehead and my cheeks. "You'll have it," he promises. "Everything you can take and then some."

I'm quivering with anticipation as I squeeze around the emptiness inside me, craving more—needing it, almost as much as I need air.

Then I feel it—his tip against me, thicker than three fingers put together, but even more welcome.

"Yes," I gasp raggedly. "Please please please—*yes!*"

He's sinking into me. The head of his cock is stretching me open almost as far as I can go, and it's so fucking good.

I can't stop myself from arching into him, pressing my

body against his as he kisses my neck and forehead and cheeks and whispers about how well I'm taking him.

Inch by inch, he pushes further into me, whispers sweet things into my ears, lets his touch wander across my body until I'm writhing with pleasure…

Just as it feels like he's stretching me almost past my limit, I feel him pull back and thrust. Every muscle in his body is rippling as he presses against me, and my world is spinning to pieces around me.

"Fuck fuck fuck fuck—" I gasp raggedly, clinging tightly to him and crying out with every thrust.

"Yes!" His grunts are hot puffs of air across my neck, low and hoarse and full of need. "Ronan. Fuck…!"

Time is slipping out of place.

Alph throws his weight onto me, pressing me into the bed as I run my nails down his back and bare my throat for his teeth. I squeeze tight around his shaft, pushing up against him as he drives into me.

His pace is faster and harder now, losing the rhythm but gaining all the more urgency. Every muscle in my body is so taut I feel like I could snap and go flying across the room— but he's pinning me down, surging into me until I don't know where he ends and I begin.

My world is narrowing until, at last, it's just me and Alph, and nothing else.

"Alph…!" I cry out, burying my face in his neck, breathing in the musk of his sweat as he pushes into me and sparks fly with every single goddamn thrust. "Oh, fuck. Fuck, Alph. I can't—I can't stop it—"

"Yes," Alph pants hoarsely into my ear. "I want everything, you hear me? I want you to cum for me, Ronan. I want to see it all."

My eyes squeeze closed as I arch off the bed, clinging to him for dear life… and then my muscles quiver and give way. The rhythm between our bodies disappears as frantic need sweeps us up and carries us over the edge together.

I'm lost to the waves of blackness, clenching hard around his cock as the heat sweeps through me. I can barely even tell if I'm crying his name out loud or in my head… but I *do* know he's moaning mine.

It feels like forever before I manage to open my eyes again. He's slipping out of me, holding me close, pressing his lips to mine over and over again.

"I love you," he breathes against my lips, holding me so tight against his body. "God, how I love you, Ronan." Then he cracks his eyes open and peers at me. "But you don't need to feel pressured to answer—"

I giggle so hard I can hardly answer, too breathless with the pure joy spilling out of me—and not just literally. It's like a light that radiates from every cell of my body.

"Oh, Alph," I whisper. "I love you, too."

I know the voyage of a lifetime is only just beginning… and I can't wait to find out where it leads.

Epilogue

RONAN — NEXT APRIL

"How does it feel to be a fully-qualified fashion designer?" Alph's brother, Felix, beams at me as he presses a glass of champagne into my hand.

Everyone keeps asking that, and my answer never changes.

"Amazing," I breathe out. "So freaking amazing."

"And," Alph leans in as if everyone doesn't already know, "a new permanent employee of XX Gracieux!"

He's even learned how to pronounce the name. I giggle and swat at his chest, but I can't lie—I'm proud as *hell*.

My own brand? Yeah, that's coming someday—perhaps someday soon. But first, I need to work my way up in the industry. I have a lot left to learn, and a whole lifetime to learn it in.

Alph's tours have been going well—better and better, in fact—so it's nice to share our downstairs office space. Together, we're figuring out all the things we don't yet know.

With the graduation ceremony over, everyone's here. Alph's brothers, and I'm proud to call them my friends now, too. My classmates, who have become frequent visitors to Sunrise Island. Half of Sunrise Island, all crammed into this little room.

And, of course, my family. They never quite know what to make of this place, and they certainly would never want to live here… but they seem to love visiting it.

That's not all. There's a guest of honour, who swore she'd only be here for two hours maximum… but Kieran's beaming smiles and plentiful glasses of champagne seem to have won her over.

"Ronan," Gabby leans in to whisper. "It's time, right?" Alph taps a fork on his glass, grinning at me, and the bar goes quiet.

Even though we've graduated, I don't think I'll ever call her by her first name.

"Professor Meyer. We can't thank you enough for every-thing you've done for us. Speaking for myself… without you, I don't think I'd be half the designer—or half the man—I am today."

"Hear, hear!"

My classmates cheer loudly enough that even Professor Meyer blushes.

I clear my throat and raise my glass. "To Professor Meyer. You didn't just see the best in each of us… you helped each of us see the best in ourselves."

She clears her throat and looks down, and we all pretend not to notice her dab her eyes.

But before I can sit back down, Alph clears his throat and puts down his glass. "There's one more thing."

"Hm?"

Felix plucks my champagne glass right out of my hand, and before I can so much as ask him why…

Alph sinks to one knee, his other knee thudding hollowly against the wooden deck under the bar.

I raise both hands to my mouth as the bar goes quiet all over again, all eyes suddenly on us.

"Ronan Ashfield. You've taught me more than I ever thought there was to know about wanting, waiting, and best of all, having."

Alph's eyes sparkle as he gazes up at me, digging out a little box. He flips it open as I gasp at the beautiful diamond, set into a silver band.

Of course he chose a classic—something that really will go with every style I might possibly want to wear.

"But I've been told there's more. There's having, and there's holding… for better, or for worse… and a lot of other words that I'm going to learn, if that's the kind of ceremony you want." Alph's grin twinkles up at me. "Because I can tell you right now… all I want is you. So, will you marry me?"

"Yes, yes, *yes!*" I gasp, flinging my arms around him as the bar erupts into applause.

Alph beams at me as he gently takes my hand to push the ring onto my finger. He turns over each of my palms and kisses them one at a time… and then he straightens up, and I leap straight into his arms.

I don't waste a moment to grab Alph by the cheek, leaning in for a good, long kiss. Because I'm not waiting on my forever anymore. It's here and now.

It's ours.

About the Author

E. Davies writes feel-good, low-angst romance that never fades to black when the going gets good! Born in Canada, after 16 moves and counting, Ed has finally put down roots in north London.

He emerges from his writing nest to coo over fuzzy animals, flee from cute guys, dance through the streets with his chosen family, put together fierce looks, and—most of all —befriend local flowers.

FOLLOW E. DAVIES ONLINE:

- amazon.com/author/edavies
- bookbub.com/authors/e-davies
- facebook.com/edaviesauthor
- goodreads.com/edavies
- instagram.com/edaviesauthor

AFTER

Afterburn, Afterglow, Aftermath

SHARED UNIVERSES

Rosavia Royals: Barely Regal

Men of Hidden Creek: Shelter, Adore, Miracle, Redemption

Vino & Veritas: Limelight

AND MORE...

For a complete list of available titles by E. Davies:

edaviesbooks.com/books